Corkscrews and Camembert

Michelle Ford

This is a work of fiction. Names, characters, places, and incidents either are the product of the author's imagination or are used factitiously, and any resemblance to any persons, living or dead, business establishments, events, or locales is entirely coincidental.

CORKSCREWS AND CAMEMBERT

Kinglet Books
Victoria BC, Canada

Cover design by GetCovers

ISBN: 978-1989677735 (print paperback)
ISBN: 978-1989677612 (ebook)
ISBN: 978-1989677759 (large print paperback)
ISBN: 978-1989677742 (print hardcover)

First edition: April 2023

Chapter 1

Brianna West sank onto her small couch and put her feet on the coffee table in contentment. Her friend Macy Jones reached forward to rescue a glass of wine from her friend's errant toes.

"Research looks like the hardest part of your job," Macy said with a sigh as she leaned back into the couch. "I don't know. How will we ever decide which wine pairs with which cheese? There's so much testing involved."

Brianna chuckled and sliced off a wedge of Camembert from the round cutting board perched between them on the couch cushions. She paired it with a salted cracker and popped it between her lips then brushed her curly brown hair away from her face.

"So hard," she agreed through her full mouth. "Pity me."

"I would, except I'm in the trenches with you." Macy took a sip of her wine. "This Camembert really does go with Merlot."

"It does, but we'll have to test it with the wines I want to serve at my wine and cheese night. Choosing Starberry Farm's Camembert as the main representative of the cheese side of things was easy, and it pairs so nicely with wine, but every wine's flavor profile is slightly different, and I want to get this right."

"Such a food snob," Macy said with a grin. "I guess

you're in the right business. Remember that stellar review of your café in the magazine a tourist brought over from Vancouver? What a boon for a foodie like you."

"Trust me, I'm happy to pair anything with cheese." Brianna chewed the last of her cracker and swallowed with a happy sigh. She had purchased her café, the Golden Moon, six months ago and had promptly started selling cheesy baked goods, something that had been a longtime dream of hers. "But if the whole point of this event is to showcase the best of our local industries, I want to do them justice. I'll source out wines from our local producers starting tomorrow."

"Do you have a list? There are only three on the island that I know of." Macy brought her left hand up to tick off the fingers of the hand holding the wine glass. "Whimsical Wines, Orca Vineyards, and Duchess Row. Unless you want to start looking at the surrounding islands."

"I'll see where I get with those three. The guests might get overwhelmed with too many choices. I can try out Whimsical Wines when I next see Troy."

As Brianna had expected, Macy sat up at the mention of Brianna's new friend. "Troy Winchester? I know it's still new, but you two are so cute together. Is it going well? Dish."

Brianna laughed even as her cheeks warmed. "It's good. We've only gone on a few dates, but he seems great. Really interested in me, caring, passionate about his winery."

"Passionate is a trait we can work with." Macy

grinned at her.

Brianna rolled her eyes. "Let's not move too fast. It still feels weird dating. Greg only died last year, and we were together for years before that. I haven't done the dating dance for eons."

"Like riding a bicycle." Macy nodded sagely. "Go over there next time to sample wines. With a little mood lighting, some good music, his alcohol…" She wiggled her eyebrows at Brianna, who nudged her with her knee.

"All right, all right, I get the picture. Enough of my love life. What about—"

A knock on the door interrupted Brianna. She rose from the couch, only slightly wobbly from the wine, and walked through her float home's main room to the front door. A sailor's knot hung in her window, and she smiled at it. She'd worked hard decorating her home when she'd moved in the spring, and now that autumn had arrived, she felt cozy and comfortable in her space. The door beckoned, and Brianna flung it open in welcome.

Alicia Marley, her float home neighbor and the only realtor in town, smiled brightly. Flaming red curls surrounded her face, and she wore a yellow and orange patterned sweater that made her look like a walking advertisement for autumn. If she'd rolled in fallen leaves prior to visiting, her colors wouldn't have been brighter.

"Brianna, I'm glad I caught you." She noticed Macy on the couch. "Is this a bad time? I can come back tomorrow."

Brianna ushered her inside. "Not at all. We were just sampling wines and cheeses. Do you know Macy Jones?"

"Of course," Alicia said with a wave. "Macy used to babysit my son Joel."

"He and Oaklyn always played well together," Macy said. "So cute. Now they're big grumpy teenagers. Not sure how that happened."

"Would you like some wine?" Brianna asked Alicia. "We're taste testing wine and cheese pairings for a special evening event I'm planning at the café. Tomorrow I'll source out wines from our local wineries, but today these bottles will have to do. Macy suggested checking out Orca, Whimsical, and Duchess."

"I didn't say to check them all out," Macy said. "Just that those were the only wineries on Driftwood Island. Don't bother meeting with Sebastian Merle at Orca Vineyards. He's an absolute terror. Rammed into my car in the parking lot last year—my parked car, mind you—and then had the gall to yell at me."

"And the ruckus he made at the town hall meeting when we were debating the new dock." Alicia shook her head. "A highly unpleasant man, to be sure. But don't let that stop you. He's incredibly particular about his wines, and the product speaks for itself. Delicious stuff. He's entering his wines in that big wine competition in a couple of weeks, and he has a good chance of winning, in my opinion. You'd be missing out if you didn't serve it, and as grumpy as Sebastian is, he wouldn't want to miss an opportunity to showcase his wines."

"Right. I remember Troy mentioning the competition," Brianna said. "Troy's the owner of Whimsical Wines."

"Troy Winchester?" Alicia asked. "Of course, he would certainly throw his hat in the ring. Whoever wins this competition gets to walk away with prize money, but more than that, a gold rating from the institute running the thing. That boosts sales big time, so I've heard."

"Sebastian's wines might be tasty, but I wouldn't want to talk with him. Better you than me." Macy finished her glass and stretched her arms over her head. "I should get home. Work tomorrow."

"I won't keep you either," Alicia said to Brianna. "I wanted to invite you to a dockside work party next Saturday. We're fixing up the roof of the paddle storage building, and the more people help, the quicker it all goes. It's a good chance to meet your neighbors, and there'll be pizza."

She looked hopefully at Brianna, who laughed.

"How could I resist the promise of new friends and pizza? That's a winning combo. I'll be there."

Brianna sat across from Troy at the Stumbling Goose the next evening. Her eyes glanced over his sandy hair, straight nose, and full lips with appreciation. He was a handsome man, but the best thing about him was the way he looked at her, like he couldn't keep a smile off his face when he saw her. It had been too long since anyone had looked at her like that.

"Busy day at the Golden Moon?" he asked before dipping a fry in ketchup and bringing it to his mouth.

"You know it. I finally found someone to work the front until Oaklyn comes in for her after-school shift. Teri is great—I think she'll run the place wonderfully while I'm baking—but training takes time, and even the most efficient worker can't know everything at the start. I barely had time to eat today, which is why this burger tastes out of this world." She dramatically dipped a fry in ketchup and brought it to her mouth to illustrate her hunger.

"Is space travel the sign of a good date?" Troy said with a sideways twist of his lips.

"I'd say so." Brianna grinned back, then nodded toward Troy. "How about you? What did you do at Whimsical Wines today?"

"Edited a few promotional videos for my website, mainly. Oh, and I finalized the wine choice for the competition in a couple of weeks. Did I tell you about that?" At Brianna's nod, Troy sighed. "It's a big deal. If I win, it will put Whimsical on the map. Restaurant deals, plugs by celebrities, you name it. If I don't, Whimsical Wines might fade into obscurity, and I've sunk too much into this business to let that happen."

Brianna grabbed his hand, moved by his anxiety. Troy squeezed it back.

"I'm sure you'll do well at the competition," she said, taking her hand back to pick up the last bite of her burger. "And surely it's not the only thing going. I mean, the Golden Moon's big wine and cheese night will be the event of the decade."

Troy chuckled at Brianna's teasing smile. "You're right, of course. But winning would pave my way, no doubt about it."

They spoke of other topics, and Brianna loved how effortlessly their conversation flowed. When it came time to pay, Brianna tried to pull out her purse, but Troy put up a firm hand.

"This one's on me," he said.

"No, I can do it," she protested. "Don't be so old-fashioned."

Troy raised an eyebrow at her. "How about you get the next one, if you agree to another date?"

Brianna's cheeks warmed and she couldn't stop her smile. She put away her purse. "That's fair. It's a promise."

She excused herself to visit the washroom while Troy chatted to the server. Upon exiting the ladies' room, she bumped into a solid figure.

"Oh, sorry," she blurted out.

"Ms. West." Corporal Devon Moore's deep voice was pleasant to her ears. His hands, which had caught her and stopped her from stumbling into the wall, weren't swift to leave her arms. Their warmth left her bare skin tingling. "You usually pride yourself on your observation skills."

Brianna put her hands on her hips, only pretending to be annoyed. She looked up at the dark-haired man whose handsome eyes still gazed at her. "Can't a girl have a night off every now and again? Besides, this island has reverted to its sleepy self, thank goodness." At his nod of agreement, she squinted at him. "You can call me Brianna, by the way. I'm not that formal."

"Brianna," he said, trying out the name. It sounded good in his smooth voice. "When I'm off the clock, Devon works for me."

He had a nice smile. His already handsome face only improved with the inviting expression.

"Devon?" A saccharine voice preceded a fine-featured woman with shiny black hair above a petite frame perched on high-heeled boots. Brianna recognized her as Cecelia Yang, who worked at the post office. Her voice sharpened when she saw Brianna, like the pointed end of a licked candy cane. "There you are. Ready to go?"

"Yes," he said. He nodded at Brianna, his eyes not leaving her face. "I'll see you tomorrow—the Mountie detachment insists on their scones."

Cecelia's smile didn't reach her eyes as she pulled Devon toward the pub's front door. Brianna shook her head, puzzled by her reaction to Devon's touch. Then she straightened her shoulders. Troy was waiting.

After the bustle of the pub, Brianna sank onto her float home's window seat with a sigh. Then she frowned. The house felt even quieter and emptier than usual, especially after a marvelous evening with Troy. She considered turning on some music to fill the silence, but that wasn't what she really wanted. She wanted a presence, someone to share her home with. The thought of cohabiting made her shake her head violently—she and Troy had only just started dating, and she wasn't sure if she was ready for any commitment after losing Greg last year—and her house wasn't large enough for a roommate, even if Brianna had wanted to share with a stranger. But what could she do?

An intriguing thought crawled into her mind, insidious and captivating. It haunted her during her evening ablutions, and by bedtime, she'd made up her mind. She fell asleep with a smile on her face, anticipating the morning.

After her baking the next day, she presented herself at the island's animal shelter.

"Do you have any cats that need a home?" she asked the woman inside, who flung her large hands wide with an expression of glee on her face.

"Yes," she said loudly. "Yes, we do. Three little furballs have been here for a few weeks and would love to find homes. Come meet them."

The woman ushered her into a room filled with kennels. With a coo, she opened the hatch to the first one and lifted out a long-haired cat with an orange back and white chin. The cat's green eyes gazed at Brianna while the animal purred in the woman's arms.

"This is Paprika," the woman said with an affectionate rub of the cat's chin. "She's three years old and very loving. She could use a good home, that's for sure."

"Hi, Paprika," Brianna said, extending her hand to

the cat to sniff. Paprika nosed her finger then pushed against her hand looking for a rub. Brianna chuckled and gave the cat a scratch behind the ears. Her eyes grew moist.

"Would you like to see the other two?" the woman said with a smile.

Brianna bit her lip. If she saw the others, she'd end up with three cats to take home. Friendly Paprika was a good start.

"I'd like to give Paprika a home, please," she said clearly. The woman passed her the cat, and Brianna gently hugged the warm animal in her arms. The cat rumbled its pleasure, and Brianna sighed. She and Paprika needed each other. She hoped the cat wouldn't mind her float home.

Chapter 2

Brianna left sweet Paprika to explore her new home while she took a quick trip to the liquor store. She was out of vodka, a crucial secret ingredient for her pastry. She'd rolled up her rugs and placed the water and litter box in prominent positions. Hopefully, Paprika would know what to do with them. She wasn't a kitten, but this was a new home for her.

Brianna picked up her pace. She would have to be quick at the store, that was all. Paprika would be fine for a half hour. It would be good for her to learn that Brianna would return. She probably wanted some solitude. She was a cat, after all.

Brianna turned up the road, strolled past the hardware store and a bakery, and strode briskly into the liquor store. Rows of bottles lined the shelves, and she walked straight to the hard liquor. She found a brand she liked and pulled it off the shelf.

Raised voices caught her attention, and she craned her neck over the nearest shelf to see what was going on. Others in the store joined her in looking for the source of the noise, and she chuckled to herself. She was turning into a nosy small-town woman. Was it a bad thing to be interested in her fellow villagers? She preferred it to the anonymity of her old big-city life.

"I expressly told you that these bottles should get front-of-the-aisle placement," a man with a hoarse voice yelled at the aproned man with thin black hair and a protruding belly behind the front counter. The cashier's wide eyes blinked behind round glasses at the angry man before him.

Brianna could only see the man's back, which was covered in plaid flannel. Close-cropped gray hair stuck out from his head in wiry bristles, and his shoulders were fixed in a permanent hunch. When he turned slightly to gesticulate, his craggy face and hooked nose became clear. Lines fell from his nose to his chin in carved furrows from years of scowling.

Brianna's mouth twisted. That was not the face of a pleasant man, and his shouting confirmed it.

"What are you going to do about it?" the unpleasant man yelled at the cashier. "Huh?"

"I'll see what I can do, but I can't make any promises," the cashier said bravely. "We have obligations for that placement."

"Bah!" The man threw up his hands and stalked out of the store. Brianna exchanged a glance with a woman in the next aisle.

"Always had a temper, Sebastian did." The older woman tutted. "I see he hasn't lost it. What a scene. And all to make sure his wines are at the front. No manners at all."

The woman ambled down the aisle, and Brianna narrowed her eyes. Was this Sebastian Merle, owner of Orca Vineyards? Despite Macy's warning, she'd planned to approach him about her wine and cheese event, but now she was reconsidering.

She squared her shoulders. She was a business owner

now, and sometimes that meant taking the bad with the good for the sake of her business. Besides, she was a big girl and could handle a grumpy old man.

Brianna's aunt Dot Dubois huffed beside her on her rickety touring bicycle that Monday morning, painted with a sponge dipped in a rainbow of colors and sporting a large wicker basket on the handlebars.

"It's been a while," Dot panted. She turned a baleful eye on the rest of the hill before them. "I'm out of shape, while you've been peddling around for months… not to mention I have twenty years on you."

"Excuses, excuses." Brianna changed gears to ease her burning legs. She took deep, calm breaths to cover her own pounding heart. "It's good for you. I'm keeping you healthy."

"Eating carrots would do the same thing," Dot grumbled, but she stopped talking to focus on getting her bike up the hill. A bike trailer rolled behind her, and Dot's miniature white goat Zola peered with interest at the passing road from a screened window.

When they crested the ridge, Brianna gazed with pleasure at the scene below them. Fields of golden hay swayed in the breeze. A few fenced pastures held black cows and a small herd of fluffy sheep. A stream wound beside the road, and on the right, rows of grapevines stood in military precision next to the gently sloping foothill of a small mountain.

Brianna soared down the empty road, Dot whooping

behind her. When they reached a large wooden sign carved with a leaping killer whale and painted the stark black and white of the marine mammal, Brianna turned right onto a gravel driveway. Long rows of grapevines stretched from the drive down a gentle slope, each row tidy and painfully straight. Beyond the vineyard stood a sprawling farmhouse. It was painted a bland beige, covered by the solar panels that were ubiquitous on this small island, and nestled in a group of Garry oaks. More prominent was the winery in a converted barn at the end of the driveway. The same killer whale insignia adorned the barn's front, accompanied by the words "Orca Vineyards."

Dot frowned at a cluster of people in front of the barn as she pulled her bike next to Brianna's. "I thought they weren't open for visitors today."

"They aren't." Brianna pointed. "Look, there's an ambulance. I wonder what happened."

"Let's find out."

Before Brianna could protest, her aunt glided forward toward the vehicles and people grouped around the winery's front door. Brianna shook her head and followed. Dot wasn't known for her subtlety.

"Excuse me," Dot said to a woman wringing her hands beside the ambulance. Her thin blond braid hung down her back, and her round face looked more prone to smiles than her current worried expression. "Is everything all right? What's all the commotion about?"

"Oh, it's terrible." The woman hugged herself, although her eyes were dry. "A picker found Sebastian. He—" She gulped, her face pale. "They found him

14

floating in a fermentation vat. Dead.”

“Oh!” Dot’s eyes widened. “I’m so sorry to hear that. We were on our way here to meet with him.”

Brianna murmured words of compassion to echo Dot’s, and the woman turned back to the barn, where emergency workers were speaking with Mounties at the scene. Her stomach roiled with queasiness. Drowned in his own wine—it was too horrible to imagine. How had it happened? Had he fallen in after imbibing his own product?

A man with long brown hair sidled up to the woman they’d spoken with and chattered quietly. Brianna held her breath to hear.

“The ventilation system was turned off.”

“Why was the system off?” the woman demanded. “Was there a power failure?”

“No idea. Carbon dioxide from the fermenting grapes must have overwhelmed Sebastian. It can get pretty thick in there if there’s no ventilation.” The man looked around and spoke more quietly. “But that’s not all. I overheard the police say it might not have been an accident. Sebastian had a head wound, and a corkscrew was on the floor next to the vat with blood on the tip.”

“Do you think someone stabbed him with it?” The woman’s eyes widened.

“It’s certainly sharp enough to kill a person. The racking cane was lying on the floor, too. And then someone shoved him into the vat? Who would do that?”

“He made enemies more easily than he made friends,” the woman replied with a sorrowful shake of her head. "But I can't believe someone would do that. I don't know, what is the world coming to?"

As the two wandered away, Brianna shuffled closer to her aunt.

"Did you hear that?" she hissed in Dot's ear. "They're saying murder, not an accident."

"Oh my." Dot glanced around the group of people as if to identify the killer. "Did karma finally bite old Sebastian? I hate to speak ill of the dead, but he was cantankerous as a young man, and he didn't age nearly as well as his wines do."

Brianna spotted Devon striding out of the barn, his face pale. She ignored the squirm in her stomach. Had he seen the body? Before she could consider her actions, she sidled toward him.

"Hi, Devon," she called.

His face brightened at her words, and he walked swiftly over to her.

"What are you doing here, Brianna?" he asked.

"I was hoping to talk to Sebastian Merle about ordering some wine for a café event I have coming up, but I heard our sleepy town had a rude awakening. Is it true? Was he hit on the head then tossed into a fermentation vat?"

His eyes widened at her knowledge, then they narrowed. "You know I can't tell you that."

"I know. But you can't blame a girl for trying."

Devon shook his head and walked away, but not before she glimpsed his barely suppressed smile.

"Stay out of it," he called over his shoulder. "You know the drill."

Brianna chuckled. She had no intention of looking into this murder. Exonerating her aunt in the spring had been enough for her. She didn't need another project, not when the police could handle this themselves. It was their job, after all.

Brianna walked back to Dot, who looked expectantly at her.

"No info from him," she said to her aunt. "But I'm glad you're not involved this time. One of your confessions is enough for me. Come on, we won't do any good gawking at the emergency workers. We came here to talk to Sebastian Merle, but that clearly can't happen now."

Brianna felt distinctly ruffled after the incident at Orca Vineyards. After she turned a corner toward the town of Snuggler's Cove, she said to Dot, "I can't believe Sebastian Merle died. What a mess."

"A tragic loss of life," Dot agreed, "and a monkey wrench in your wine and cheese event plans."

"Need some tea after that fuss?"

"Oh, yes. And one of your blueberry cream cheese scones." Dot smacked her lips. "That will do nicely."

They wheeled into the gravel alley beside the Golden Moon. Brianna noted the weeds in the gravel and wondered if she should pull them. Later, she decided. Tea with her aunt held far more appeal, and she had a wine and cheese event to plan. Winter would arrive soon enough and halt the weeds' growth.

Dot led Zola out of her trailer and tied her rope securely to a drainpipe. Brianna watched with interest.

"Do you use a bowline?" she asked her aunt. "That's smarter than me. I used a loose reef knot, which Zola Houdini escaped from. She ate half a cheese platter."

Dot howled with laughter, and Zola bleated at the sound.

"Sorry, my love." Dot squatted to give the little goat a head rub. "I didn't mean to scare you. I was laughing at your antics. You gave your poor cousin Brianna a runabout, did you?" With a final chuckle, she scratched Zola's ear then stood and turned to Brianna. "Lead the way, darling. I'm parched."

Brianna walked through the front door of her café. Every time she entered the space, her heart filled to bursting with pride and love. The yellow walls glowed brightly, and the floor and tables gleamed with warm wood tones. Pictures of cheeses surrounded by vintage frames dotted the walls, and her display of antique cheese knives hung in pride of place above a cheery electric fireplace. Customers lounged at their tables, eating and chatting happily.

Oaklyn, Macy's teenage daughter, stood behind the espresso machine with a look of concentration on her face. Her dyed black hair was pulled up in a ponytail— at Brianna's insistence, given her role in food handling—but her eyeliner was as thick as ever, and the numerous silver cuffs on her ears glinted in the overhead lights.

She looked a bit like a hooligan, in Brianna's opinion, but so far she'd been an excellent employee—

at least, once Brianna had trained her to greet customers with a friendly expression. Brianna now trusted her to look after the café for short periods during her afternoon shifts, especially since Annalise, her neighbor at the yarn shop, had agreed to help in case of an emergency.

"Everything going okay, Oaklyn?" she asked the girl when she slipped behind the counter to join her.

Oaklyn shrugged. "It's good. Busy enough. We're almost out of gougères."

Brianna glanced at a clock on the wall. "It's too late to make more and have them sell. Just say we're out when they're gone. That will teach people not to dither about or wait to buy later in the day when they could buy earlier."

A swift grin crossed Oaklyn's face. Then a crease of worry formed in her smooth forehead.

"What's the matter?" Brianna asked. "Anything I can help with?"

"No," Oaklyn said with a sigh. "I just can't figure out what to wear tomorrow. Oh, can I leave the café early in the afternoon?"

"That should be fine." Brianna mentally checked her calendar. "Yes, that's fine. What's the occasion?"

"A boy at school, Rob. We're going to meet at the pizza place for an early dinner. Kind of like a date, I guess."

"Oh." Brianna eyed the younger girl. "That's exciting. What are you thinking?"

"I don't know." Oaklyn dragged the last word out in a frustrated whine. "I want to look good, obviously, but

I don't want to look like I'm trying too hard. It's just the pizza place, you know? But it's also a date. Sort of. I think. What if he doesn't think it's a date? And then I show up wearing something too nice, and he thinks I had the wrong idea, and it would be so embarrassing."

That was the longest string of words Oaklyn had ever uttered in Brianna's presence. She blinked, trying to decide how to respond. She didn't want to squander this opportunity when Oaklyn was clearly opening up.

"Well," she said slowly, "ball gowns are out, but so are your work clothes." Oaklyn threw her a look of exasperation, so Brianna quickly said, "Honestly, the best thing you can wear is confidence. You could dress in a toga, but if you hold your head high and strut around like you own the place, others would line up to buy their own togas."

"Yeah, okay." Oaklyn didn't look impressed. "But I'm not going to wear a toga."

"My point is, wear something that you feel comfortable in. That will help with your confidence, and then what you have on will matter less."

Oaklyn looked thoughtful. A customer approached, and she turned to deal with him. Brianna took a teapot off the shelf and filled it. She hid her smile from the girl. It had been a while since she'd dealt with boy troubles. Now she had man troubles, although they weren't such a trouble at the moment. Troy was shaping up to be an excellent companion.

Brianna slid two blueberry cream cheese scones onto a plate and balanced it on her palm while she walked over to Dot. Her aunt brightened at her arrival.

"Pass those scones over here," she said with grabby hands. "Yes, my darlings. You'll be in my mouth soon enough."

Brianna chuckled and set down their tea things. "Sorry I took a while. I was chatting with Oaklyn about her boy troubles. She's on a date tomorrow night and can't decide what to wear." Brianna frowned. "Well, she was unclear about whether or not it was a date. I hope this Rob character treats her well. He'd better show up."

"Ah, young love." Dot sloshed tea into her teacup. "Such a tumultuous time, but so glorious. So much to learn. And then when you're an old biddy like me, you know everything, but the men are a little thinner on the ground." Dot held up her teacup in a toast. "To love in all its stages."

Brianna clinked her teacup with Dot's, thinking of Troy with a smile. "I'll toast to that."

Dot gulped her tea, and then her gaze turned toward the door. "Speak of the devil, and he shall appear," she said to Brianna with a wink.

Brianna turned. Troy was silhouetted against the bright sunshine outside the café, and her heart lurched pleasantly. She stood and walked toward him, and he gave her a lopsided smile.

"I was passing by." He motioned toward the gleaming black motorbike at the curb with a gloved hand. "I thought I'd pop in to say hi."

"That was sweet of you." A strange scent of burned grass wafted past her, and she wrinkled her nose. What had Troy walked through? "Can I get you a coffee or something? On the house, of course."

"I'm fine, thanks. Can't stay long. Lots going on."

"Busy prepping for the competition? It's in a couple of weeks, isn't it?"

"Yeah, that's it." His voice brightened. "It's really stressing me out, but I'm sure it will all turn out in the end. Just have to get through this pre-show busyness."

"Well, if there's anything I can do to help, just say the word." Brianna held her breath, waiting to see how he would respond. Bah, she was as bad as Oaklyn, fretting over what her "boy" was going to say. She squared her shoulders and released the air from her lungs deliberately.

"You're doing it." Troy smiled. "It's great to see you. I should get going, but I'm looking forward to our next date."

Brianna grinned. "Me too."

Chapter 3

Magnus Pickleton rapped on the folding table, his bristly gray beard quivering with indignation that the group didn't immediately fall silent with rapt attention. Hilda Button tittered at something Esme Alonso said, her darning needle ceaselessly flicking in and out of the teal sock she was mending. Quentin Flagstaff's head was studiously buried in his meeting notes above a natty red bowtie.

Brianna slid into her seat, greeted with a smile from Esme and a scowl from Magnus.

"Now that we are all finally here," he said, "the September meeting of Driftwood Island's Gourmand Society can start. To begin, food-related news on the island. As you all know, Snuggler's Cove has the tremendous honor of hosting the British Columbia Wine Association's industry competition this year. The council has taken control of the proceedings." Magnus sniffed at the audacity of the township's council to wrest the opportunity away from his society. "It will take place at the hall—right here—and there are plenty of opportunities to volunteer. Let's all support our stellar local wineries."

"Speaking of local wines, my wine and cheese event at the Golden Moon is coming up shortly," Brianna piped up. "I'm in the process of pairing my selections, all sourced locally, of course. I'm open to suggestions from my fellow gourmands.”

“How lovely,” Hilda said. “I do enjoy a special event. I’ll be sure to come.”

“I’ve found that a sharp cheddar goes splendidly with Orca Vineyards’ Cabernet Sauvignon,” Quentin offered. “Along with some chutney, too.”

“Noted.” Brianna smiled at Quentin. “Thanks for the suggestion. I’ll be highlighting Starberry Farm’s Camembert for this event, but a few other cheeses on the side would be welcome, I imagine.”

“You can’t forget the fine chèvres from Foxwood Farm,” Magnus said with outrage, his beard quivering. “And to completely ignore Porter Island’s Dewdrop Dairy? Their cheeses are an excellent example of local artisan products. It would be a grave error to ignore them, even if they are from a neighboring island.”

“I don’t mind compiling a list of local cheeses that would pair well with wine,” Quentin added.

“I have the cheese side in hand—” Brianna said, feeling a little panicky about how the Gourmand Society was running away with her event ideas.

“And I was speaking to Billie from Foxwood just the other day,” said Hilda. She nodded thoughtfully, her white curled hair bobbing with the motion. “I’m sure I could convince her to help sponsor your event. Leave it to me, dear.”

Brianna opened her mouth to protest, but Esme saved her with a wink.

“While thinking of ideas for Brianna’s cheese event is great fun,” Esme said to the rest with a raised eyebrow, “is no one going to mention yesterday’s death? Are we all so inured to dead bodies that Sebastian Merle's demise isn't noteworthy?"

"I hardly think that Sebastian's tragedy is relevant to Gourmand Society proceedings," said Magnus with a huff.

"Magnus, Magnus, Magnus," Esme said with a shake of her head. "Sebastian Merle was a cornerstone of the food scene on Driftwood. Orca Vineyards is an established winery, and you can find its wines in every restaurant on Driftwood and the surrounding islands. What happened to its founder is crucial to the Gourmand Society."

Hilda nodded. "Well said, my dear. Quite right. And it's such a terrible story, him being stabbed in the head and thrown into a vat of wine. What an untimely end."

"They're saying it's murder, aren't they?" Quentin added. "Any idea who?"

"Well." Hilda's needle slowed as she considered the topic. "Who, indeed? The enemies of Sebastian Merle are many."

"That's the truth." Esme leaned back in her chair. "You won't find me shedding any tears for him. But to brain him and push the body into a vat?" She shuddered, and her huge golden hoop earrings jiggled with the motion. "That's an end I wouldn't wish on my worst enemy."

Quentin finished his note then put down his pen. "What about his wine competitors? Whimsical Wines is giving Orca a run for its money. Is there bad blood between them?"

"Sebastian's blood was as bad as it got, but I don't

know of a particular beef between the two besides general competitive rivalry," said Magnus.

"I'm sure Whimsical Wines had nothing to do with it." Brianna leaped to Troy's defense, her stomach twisting uncomfortably at the suggestion of his potential involvement in murder. She'd dealt with that after her aunt's false confession in the spring.

"I'm sure you're right, dear." Hilda patted Brianna's hand. "Young Troy is a sweet man."

"Brianna would know all about that," Esme said with a knowing glance. Brianna's cheeks warmed, and Esme snickered.

"If we have nothing else to discuss besides unfounded speculations about the murder, then let's continue with our meeting," Magnus said sternly. "Today, I will give a brief presentation on the history of Camembert."

Brianna settled in to listen to Magnus's rambling lesson—most notably that Camembert used to have a blue-gray rind instead of the modern pure white—but her mind was half on Troy. Did he know others were idly pointing fingers in his direction? She should let him know so he could be on his guard against the rumor mill.

Brianna called Troy on her walk home from the Gourmand Society meeting. He picked up after the third ring, and she sighed happily at his "hello."

"Hi, Troy," she said. "Just checking in, seeing how

you're doing."

"Not bad, not bad." His voice held a hint of strain. "Busy prepping for this competition. But I'm looking forward to our next date."

Brianna grinned. "Me too." She remembered the reason she'd called Troy and waffled over bringing up the society's suspicions. She decided to feel him out.

"Did you hear about Sebastian Merle's death yesterday? They're saying it's murder."

"Yeah, I heard." Troy sighed heavily. A rustling noise sounded like he'd switched the phone to his other ear. "Terrible news. I'm worried that the police are going to come to my door since I'm his main business competitor. It's what I'd do if I were law enforcement."

"I'm sure there are others with motivations. Pointing fingers at the competition feels pretty weak to me." Brianna decided not to mention the Gourmand Society's musings. She didn't want to upset Troy any further.

"I spoke with Sebastian that morning at his vineyard," Troy said. "I don't know. What if they draw the wrong conclusions from that? We stayed outside the whole time, but still, I wouldn't want them to get the wrong idea."

Brianna's mouth twisted with anxiety, and she took a deep breath to calm herself. "If anyone knocks on your door, just work with them, and tell the truth. Everything will come out in the wash."

"What if you come to my door?" Troy said in a teasing tone. "Do we have to stick to work topics?"

Brianna's smile colored her words. "I'm sure we can

discuss other things. Like how I need to test some of your wine for my event."

"That sounds like a great premise for a date. Friday night at my place?"

"I'll bring the cheese."

The next afternoon, Brianna was wiping off the butcher block in the café kitchen when a familiar voice drifted in from the dining room. Brianna's hands slowed momentarily, but then she scrubbed even harder at a stubborn crumb stuck to the wood. She would go out and greet him when she was ready. It was important to be social with her customers, but he didn't need any special attention.

Devon looked as handsome as ever in his Mountie uniform. He spoke with Oaklyn behind the counter but quickly glanced Brianna's way when she ducked through the open doorway into the dining room. A smile flashed over his face, and Brianna couldn't help returning it.

"You're late today," she said. "Your fellow officers must be getting after you for their treats."

"Busy morning. But morale is low without our Wednesday morning scone break, that's for sure. I'm here to make up the shortfall." He scanned the glass-fronted counter. "Looks like slim pickings this late in the day."

"Early bird gets the worm." Had she really just said that? How inane.

"Luckily, I don't want worms." Devon's eyes crinkled at the corners. "And the second mouse gets the cheese. So, here I am."

She chuckled and then moved closer to the counter. "I've got this, Oaklyn. Could you wipe down tables now?"

Oaklyn nodded. She grabbed a spray bottle and cloth with her typical teenage lassitude and wandered among the tables. Brianna grabbed a cardboard box from behind her and loaded it up with cheese scones from the display cabinet.

"I'll be glad when this week is over." Devon rolled his neck and shoulders. "The weather is too nice to be stuck inside working. My poor boat is getting lonely without me."

"A boat?" Brianna was intrigued. "Where do you keep it docked?"

"My place is on the lake," he explained. "I have a dock. And the boat is only a rowboat with a tiny electric motor I added last month. Hardly a yacht. But it's great for fishing."

Brianna closed the box lid over her perfectly golden cheese scones and ripped off a piece of tape from a nearby dispenser to keep it closed. "What kind of fish do you catch?"

"Trout, mainly. I think the council stocks the lake with them. They're tasty smoked."

"Oh, smoked trout with herbed cream cheese? Absolutely divine."

They grinned at each other.

"I can bring you some, if you like," Devon said.

"Kingfishers bring presents of fish to their potential mates," Oaklyn muttered as she passed by on her way to the kitchen.

Devon coughed, and his cheeks colored slightly. Brianna pushed the scone box toward him.

"There we are," she said loudly. Her voice had a little too much pep for the occasion. "Your scones. I hope the other officers enjoy them."

"They always do." Devon pushed some cash toward her and carefully grasped the box. "See you around."

Devon strode out of the café, and Brianna watched him go. She was grateful that he had ignored Oaklyn's comment. Teenagers could be so awkward and out of place. Brianna was only being friendly to a customer. It wasn't as if she and Devon had anything going on between them. They were both dating other people, for pity's sake.

"Was that comment necessary?" she said quietly when she poked her head into the kitchen. A few other customers sat at tables in the front, and she didn't want them to hear their conversation.

"What do you mean?" Oaklyn turned wide, innocent eyes on Brianna, and she sighed. The girl was too good at pretending. Brianna would let it slide this time. She didn't really want to delve into whatever Oaklyn thought she'd noticed.

"Nothing. Hey, are you still planning on leaving early today? You have your date with Rob, don't you?"

Oaklyn's face fell, and she scuffed her chunky black boot against the tiles of the floor.

"No," she said glumly. "Rob can't make it. He said

he has to wash his dad's car tonight. We're meeting up tomorrow night instead."

Brianna narrowed her eyes. Washing a car? That was the weakest excuse she'd ever heard and too obvious by far. Experience would teach Oaklyn how to read the motivations of others. If she had to guess, Rob had received another invitation that had sounded more appealing than a date with Oaklyn. The two weren't officially a couple, whatever that meant to a fifteen-year-old. Was Rob bored with Oaklyn already?

If so, Oaklyn was well shot of him, but Brianna's heart ached for the hurt to come. Oaklyn, while prickly and slow to respond to her requests, wasn't as much of a bad girl as she liked to pretend. She put on a good show, but when someone needed her, she was always there. Macy had told Brianna that Oaklyn had taken responsibility for all her own expenses around the house once she'd started her job, and she'd even bought Macy a ring she thought she'd like. It was a cheap piece of jewelry from the local pharmacy, but Macy wore it proudly, and the act had gone a long way toward Brianna warming up to the girl.

"You're welcome to take off early anyway," Brianna said gently. "Up to you."

"It's fine." Oaklyn shrugged and then adjusted her apron over her yellow café tee shirt. Her black hair was a stark contrast to the bright color. "I got it."

Chapter 4

Brianna rolled into Dot's driveway on her cherry red bicycle the next morning after finishing her baking duties. Fields surrounded Dot's small acreage, and gentle slopes carpeted in coniferous trees gathered like embracing arms on the edges.

She took a deep breath of crisp autumn air, scented with cut hay, sea breezes, and a mild-but-unmistakable barnyard smell. She glanced with a grin over the white slat fence at Zola, Dot's small white goat. Zola was a pet, through and through, as much as Dot liked to pretend otherwise.

Zola bleated at Brianna, and she waved back.

"I hear you've been a naughty goat," she called out, "wrecking your fence. Don't worry. We'll fix it for you. No magical escaping this time around."

Zola stared at her with unblinking yellow eyes. Then she bent her head with studied nonchalance and snipped off some grass. Brianna chuckled and rolled her bicycle to Dot's front door.

She flicked the kickstand and left her bike on the gravel in front of the house. Gathering a tin filled with baked goods from the bike basket, she then traipsed up the sagging front steps. With a pat for the ceramic elephant standing guard, Brianna knocked on the shiny black door three times and let herself in.

"Hello?" she called out. "Anyone home?"

"Brianna, darling." Her aunt glided out of a hallway with her arms outstretched and her voluminous sleeves catching the air like a parachute. "You're here. Give us a kiss."

Brianna dutifully hugged her aunt and kissed her smooth cheek. When she stepped back, she glanced critically at Dot's choice of clothing. "I thought I was here for a work party, not a fancy afternoon tea."

"These are my work clothes!" Dot looked scandalized but spoiled the effect with a wink. "Always dress your best. What would Zola think if I turned up in a ratty old tee shirt?"

Brianna tugged at the bright orange of her aunt's dangling sleeve. The soft linen felt wonderful between her fingers. "She'd probably be disappointed that there wasn't more to chew."

Dot let out a belly laugh and took Brianna's tin from her. "More baking, I presume? But we need to earn it. Connor should be coming to help, too. Oh look. There he is."

The sound of a car engine roared louder and then cut into silence. Brianna peeked her head out the door.

Dot had put her son Connor Pearce up for adoption when he was a baby and she a frightened teenager, but the two had recently reunited. He was climbing out of his old beater, a brown sedan with rust crawling along the door edges. Brianna waved at her cousin.

"Come to muck out Zola's stall? What we do for family, right?"

Connor shielded his eyes against the sun and grinned shyly. Now that he'd lived on the island for a few months, working at the hardware store, he was slowly losing his hard-edged, rough-and-tumble looks. Nothing could erase the premature crow's feet, but the lines around his mouth now creased from more frequent smiles, and the hunted look in his eyes was fading into a modicum of trust, at least for his cousin.

"Just spending quality time with my stepsister," he joked. "Dot's hairier child."

Brianna laughed and walked down the steps, closely followed by Dot. Dot jogged to Connor and flung her arms around him.

"I have so much love to give, darling," she said once she'd released her son. "There is plenty of room in my heart for you, Brianna, and Zola."

Connor looked at the ground, but a pleased look crossed his face before he had a chance to hide it.

"Should we get started?" he said to change the subject. "I thought the fence was in a bad way."

"Oh, it is, it is." Dot ushered them across the gravel driveway and toward Zola's pasture. When Brianna drew closer, she understood her aunt's words. Two of the slats were hanging by a few splinters, and the whole side desperately needed a fresh coat of paint.

"Wood, saws, screws, screwdriver." Dot pointed at a pile of materials and tools on the ground next to the fence. "And paint. I think I have everything we need to keep Houdini in her field."

Connor picked up a crowbar and marched to the fence to remove the broken slats. Brianna hefted a wooden board. Dot picked up the electric screwdriver, but when Zola came over to investigate, Dot squatted down to give her goat a head rub.

"I think we're the only ones on duty," Brianna murmured to Connor. Connor glanced at his mother and smiled, shaking his head. Zola was now chewing on Dot's sleeves, just as Brianna had predicted, but Dot only laughed and petted Zola's head.

Connor held the boards while Brianna screwed them into place. A crisp breeze lifted the hair at her neck and cooled her down on this warm autumn day. Connor whistled tunelessly as he worked, and an expression of peace wreathed his face. Brianna was glad to see it.

"It looks lovely, darlings!" Dot said some time later. She approached the new fence boards with a paintbrush dripping with white paint. "And now, the finishing touches."

Brianna and Connor stepped back to make room for the artist to work. Zola sidled up to Brianna and nibbled at her shirt hem.

"Stop it, you goof," she said with a laugh and yanked the shirt away from Zola's sharp teeth. "I only have so many shirts."

"You have some fancy shindig coming up at your café, don't you?" Connor said suddenly. "Some cheese thing."

"A wine and cheese event," she replied, pushing Zola gently away. "Showcasing the island's artisans. I hope you can make it."

"I expect so," he said without looking at her, although his mouth twitched with pleasure at being asked.

"Your fancy man will be there, won't he?" Dot

whirled around, flecks of paint flying across the pasture. She brandished the brush at Brianna. "I'll be wanting an introduction. Make sure it happens."

"Haven't you met Troy before?" Brianna was a little surprised. Although enough people inhabited the island that not everyone knew everyone, Dot was well-connected. "He's been on the island for five years now."

"And I'll be happy to make his acquaintance." Dot waggled her eyebrows at Brianna and turned back to her painting. "I assume you'll be showcasing his wines?"

"Of course." Speaking of Troy reminded Brianna of his recent troubles. "He's in a bit of a pickle, though. He's worried that he's a suspect in the Sebastian Merle murder case since they're business rivals. I know it's making him anxious, even though he's putting on a brave face."

Dot's usually cheerful face grew grim. "Oh, I hope they sort it out. I wouldn't wish a detention center on anyone, least of all your new beau. Hopefully, it won't come to that."

"I hope they wouldn't convict the wrong person so easily," Brianna said. A lump formed in her gut.

"It happens." Connor threw an expressive glance at his mother, who nodded without her usual verve. Only a few months ago, Dot had been incarcerated, awaiting trial for a crime she hadn't committed.

"I have faith that justice will prevail." Brianna said the words aloud more to convince herself than anything. "Now, who's ready for tea? I think we've earned it by now. I brought scones."

"Do they have cheese in them?" Connor asked with a straight face and a twinkle in his eye.

Brianna wandered into the café's dining room the next morning. Sun streamed through the café's front windows and turned the yellow walls a deeper golden. The silver hair of Hilda Button glinted in the light as she waited for the customer ahead of her to finish placing his order with her new employee Teri. Teri's cheery greeting and bright-eyed smile made every customer feel like they were in good hands. Brianna smiled in welcome and moved to help her acquaintance.

"Hilda, hello. What can I get you today?"

"Hello, dear. One of your mascarpone croissants, of course, and a nice cup of tea."

Once Hilda had paid, Brianna waved toward the rest of the dining room. "Find yourself a seat, and I'll bring your things right out."

"What a sweetheart." Hilda tottered off, and Brianna bustled around fetching a teapot. When she was ready, she headed over to the elderly lady, who had pulled out her latest project and was darning away on a brilliant fuchsia sock with green polka dots. Her large silver needle flashed in a shaft of sunlight.

"Just what I needed." Hilda smiled at Brianna as she unloaded her tray of tea and all the accoutrements. "Thank you, dear."

"How is the Bumblebee this week?" Brianna asked

after the bed-and-breakfast that Hilda owned. Her daughter ran most of the day-to-day operations, but Brianna knew Hilda took a keen interest in how the Bumblebee was run, just as she took a keen interest in everything on Driftwood Island.

"Just peachy, my dear. My daughter Rosy is trying out a new dish in the restaurant, some kind of newfangled eggs benedict. It's proving quite popular."

"I'll have to come in and try it soon," Brianna said. Hilda beamed at her. The B and B's restaurant didn't serve fancy fare, as one or two members of the Gourmand Society had sniffily pointed out to Brianna in the past, but she enjoyed the classic flavors and hearty portions offered.

"Do you have a minute?" Hilda patted the seat next to her. "I have some news for you."

Hilda was always a reliable source for gossip—true or not never seemed to matter for her, as long as it was juicy and she knew it first—so Brianna sat with wary interest. She'd learned that keeping up with the Snuggler's Cove news was an important part of small-town life.

"First, how is your young Troy Winchester faring?" Hilda asked with a sympathetic eye.

Brianna absentmindedly drew a circle on the table with her finger. Did Hilda's news have something to do with him?

"He's okay," she said. "Busy with preparations for the wine competition. Oh, and he's not mine. We just started dating."

Hilda winked at her and sipped her tea. "Of course.

But still, I wanted you to know first. Bertrand, Maggie Firth's son, saw Troy leaving Orca Vineyards the fateful morning of Sebastian Merle's murder." Her mouth twisted with worry. "And I chatted with Patty from the Mountie detachment when I was dropping off my granddaughter at preschool this morning." Macy had told Brianna that Hilda liked to arrive early for drop-off and then hang around until all the children were present, just to gather whatever tidbits of gossip she could. "She told me that the police are looking into Sebastian's murder, and that anyone with a reasonable connection to him is a suspect. I'm afraid that it doesn't look good for Troy, given that he's a main business rival. Not to mention what Bertrand saw."

Hilda patted Brianna's frozen hand on the table, her brow furrowed with sympathy. Brianna stared at their hands, her mind whirling. Hilda's information that Troy had been seen leaving Orca Vineyards that morning was nothing new, but was that what everyone on the island thought? That Troy had done it, or at least was a prime suspect?

"I don't believe it for a minute," Hilda said, releasing Brianna's hand and picking up her croissant. "Troy is a fabulous young man. A pillar of our town. And once the police sort out this mess, I'm sure the terrible rumors will die down. Eventually."

A timer rang shrilly from the open kitchen door. Brianna leaped up, relieved that it had saved her from this troubling conversation.

"I need to fetch that," she said to Hilda. "Thanks for the news, and enjoy your croissant."

With automatic motions, Brianna strode past Teri at the counter and entered the kitchen, where she grabbed a clean towel. She pulled open the door of her temperamental oven—thankfully working for the past month since she had replaced the thermostat—and pulled out a large tray of ham and cheese muffins. Once those landed on the butcher block, Brianna rested her palms beside the tray and hung her head.

Troy had been in the wrong place at the wrong time, and now he had a target on his back. What would happen if the police discovered that he'd been the last one to see Sebastian Merle? What if the killer had left no evidence or Troy was being framed for the murder? Would he be wrongfully accused and sent to a detention center?

Brianna's stomach churned. Shades of Dot's wrongful incarceration in the early summer haunted her thoughts. How would this end for Troy? He had a life, a good business, and a promising future. Not to mention the bud of their growing relationship. Brianna didn't know where they were going, but she wanted to find out, without a set of bars between them.

She took a deep breath and lifted her head. She needed to think objectively. Could Troy be the killer? Had she read him wrong the past few weeks that they'd been dating?

He'd never given her a moment's doubt. Compared to her late husband Greg, Troy had been nothing but kind and supportive, not to mention fun to be around. And in every way, he'd been honest and forthright. Brianna hadn't realized how highly she prized those attributes until Troy had treated her like she was worthy of being told the truth.

He hadn't even hesitated before telling her that he'd visited Sebastian the morning of the murder. If he'd been the culprit, wouldn't he have tried to hide that fact?

Brianna shook her head and stood up straight. No, Troy wasn't the murderer. She grabbed a spatula and slid it in beside a muffin to loosen it from the pan. Then she flipped it onto a cooling rack. The problem was that the whole town thought he was the killer—or, at least, they would once Hilda finished her rounds. And with no other evidence to go on, the police might think that, too.

Brianna slapped her palm on the counter. If she wanted Troy's name cleared, it was up to her to help the investigation. When her aunt had been convicted, Brianna had been the only one willing to dig deep enough to uncover the truth. She couldn't rely on anyone else to solve this puzzle, not if she wanted to make sure Troy was in the clear.

Brianna was on the case.

Chapter 5

After Hilda's disquieting news about Troy's standing in the community and Brianna's conviction that she should investigate, she was ready for her date with Troy that evening. She wanted to confirm that he'd had nothing to do with Sebastian Merle's death. Doing so over a meal of wine and cheese was a bonus.

Brianna biked out of the marina parking lot and rode through the town of Snuggler's Cove. She waved at Annalise who was hanging over the balcony rails in her suite above the yarn shop, two long sandy braids dangling past her shoulders. Brianna rode out of town along the road leading south, past a cidery, stands of thick conifers, and a lumber yard silent in the early evening. Dusk was falling, and Brianna switched on her headlight for safety.

She turned down a side road and wheeled through the wooded roadway until she passed a sign for Whimsical Wines. Following Troy's directions, she ignored that entrance and instead turned into the next dirt driveway that led to a trim white bungalow with a well-kept lawn. A black motorcycle was tucked under the eaves. Behind the house, rows of grapes stretched across the fields.

Troy appeared moments after her knock on his forest-green door. He looked tired, with dark circles under his eyes, but he smiled warmly when he saw Brianna.

"There you are." He pulled the door open wide and ushered her in. When she passed close to him, he leaned forward and gave her a swift kiss on the lips in greeting. Brianna smiled as she returned his gesture. It had been too long since someone had greeted her with such intimate familiarity. She and Greg had stopped kissing months—years—before he'd died. She'd missed it.

When they stepped apart, Brianna held up a cloth bag that she'd pulled out of her bike's basket. "I brought cheese. And crackers. And grapes. Since I was supposed to pay for this meal, remember?"

Troy grinned. "But you have to let me provide the drinks."

"Of course." Brianna allowed him to help her out of her jacket. The breeze was chilly now that the sun was setting. Winter was making its imminent arrival known in the crisp undertone of the night wind that swept through Snuggler's Cove, even though the summer's heat still presided over the days.

"Besides," she continued once Troy closed the door and led her into the living room, "I need to test which cheese goes with which of your wines. This is a work event, didn't you know? I expect results."

"I hope I live up to your exacting standards." Troy chuckled and waved her toward the couch. "Let me grab some plates and glasses."

Brianna sat on the couch, a square, gray affair that was more comfortable than it looked, and gazed around with avid curiosity. Picture windows gave an excellent view of the vineyard outside, and trim blinds took the place of curtains. A gas fireplace flickered in the corner, and a rug with gray and black swirls lay underfoot. Brianna nodded approvingly at a floor-to-ceiling built-in bookcase that took up one entire wall, and she vowed to wander over there at some point in the evening to examine Troy's taste in books.

By the time Brianna had finished scanning the room from her perch on the couch, Troy was back with two wine glasses expertly balanced in one hand and two plates and some napkins in the other. He'd already lined up three bottles of wine with the Whimsical Wines label on the coffee table next to a corkscrew.

Troy joined Brianna on the couch, and she let him uncork his bottles while she arranged cheeses and other nibbles on a cutting board she'd brought. When their hands brushed accidentally, they smiled at each other, and Brianna's stomach fluttered.

"The merlot first," Troy said with confidence, pouring some into each wine glass. "What sort of cheese should we pair with it?"

"Definitely the Gorgonzola to start." Brianna cut them each a healthy slice of creamy blue cheese with her favorite mother-of-pearl inlaid cheese knife, laid each slice on a rye cracker, and handed one to Troy. He passed her a wine glass.

"To a successful wine and cheese event," Troy said.

"And a successful competition," Brianna responded. "May your wines shine above the rest."

They drank and tasted their cheeses.

"That's nice," Troy said after a moment of savoring. "Really nice."

"Nice is good, but I want spectacular. Let's try the sharp cheddar next."

Troy sipped his wine while Brianna cut him a slice of pungent cheddar. She debated speaking about Hilda's rumors. After all, didn't he have a right to know what the town was saying about him? She would want to know if it were her.

"Talk of the town is that it's looking dicey for you," she said. Sometimes she wished she had Macy's subtle touch in speaking of delicate subjects, but she didn't have her friend's gift of the gab. "Honestly, I'm worried for you. Have the police approached you yet?"

Troy released a massive sigh and leaned his head back. "Yes, for sure. I'm a prime suspect, but they don't have any evidence, so they haven't arrested me yet. I'm supposed to stay in town until things clear up, of course." He swirled his wine and stared at it with a gloomy expression. "I don't know what else to do. I know it looks bad. I was at Orca that morning, and Sebastian and I had an argument outside his converted barn. Although that wasn't odd. Every time I had to speak to that cantankerous old man, it always ended in a shouting match."

"From the sounds of it, you weren't the only one," Brianna said. "You should have seen the fuss he made in the liquor store last week. I've never seen anyone so quick to offend."

"Exactly. If they want to arrest me because I argued with him, then their list of suspects will be a kilometer long."

"What did you fight about?" Brianna asked. She supposed it didn't really matter, not now that Sebastian was dead, but she was still curious. Maybe whatever they had fought about would relate to what Sebastian had done next—and who he'd seen. Could his argument with Troy have led Sebastian to the killer somehow?

"Just about the competition," Troy said. "I wanted to know what wines he was putting in—I thought it would be sensible to have one or two varieties each that weren't in direct competition, just so we could both have a chance for a win—but he flew off the rails. Screamed that I was trying to pry secrets out of him, that I wanted to win by cheating, and on and on. I stopped listening after a while and left to go to the grocery store. It was too much to handle." Troy's mouth turned downward. "But I didn't kill Sebastian."

"No, of course not." Brianna put a comforting hand on his forearm. "And nobody who knows you would believe it. I—"

"Let's not talk about Sebastian Merle anymore," Troy interrupted. "I'm tired of thinking about him. What's this next cheese?" He popped a slice of Emmental into his mouth and chewed.

Brianna allowed Troy to change the subject, although the mystery of Sebastian's murder still percolated in the back of her mind. It was too bad Troy was so upset about it, but that was understandable. She wanted to discuss the case with him, brainstorm who else might be a suspect, but she recognized why he didn't want to talk about it. On top of the police watching him, he had his upcoming competition. It was a stressful time for him. Maybe when she had some more concrete good news to share about the case, she would approach him again.

They had an enjoyable night tasting wines and pairing the right cheeses with them. Troy's pinched look disappeared, and he grew more relaxed with the wine and the company.

"These are going to be amazing at my event." Brianna leaned back against the couch and sipped at the dregs of a Chardonnay in her glass. "People are going to be talking up your wines, for sure."

"And hopefully returning the next day to buy your baked goods," Troy added with a clink of his wine glass against hers.

"And that. You know, you're going to sweep the board with these at your competition." Brianna flung her arm out to illustrate her point. The world felt a little fuzzy around the edges, but in a good way. Troy's wines were very easy to drink. "Gold medals all around."

"I hope Esme Alonso and the other judges agree with you," Troy said with a smile.

"Esme is judging?" Brianna narrowed her eyes at Troy. "I know her. She's in the Gourmand Society with me."

"She's a good egg. No love lost between her and Sebastian, though. I bet she's glad she doesn't have to deal with him at the competition anymore. He blew up at her once after she described his wines in one of her magazine articles as full-bodied, but with a hint of sharpness." Troy laughed in disbelief. "I mean, he was lucky she even mentioned his wines at all. I'd do anything for that sort of exposure. He didn't know how good he had it." He took a gulp of wine and looked nauseated. "Well, I guess he's not so lucky now."

Brianna swirled the last of her wine in her glass. Esme was a judge at the competition. She could have predicted that, she supposed. Esme liked to tell everyone about her famous connections in the foodie world. Either she'd been asked to be a judge or, more likely, had wheedled her way onto the panel.

Either way, Troy's comment about Esme's history with Sebastian was illuminating. Brianna didn't believe Esme had killed Sebastian, not really, but it couldn't hurt to snoop a little.

She'd have to do it carefully, though. Brianna had accused Esme of murder before. They'd managed to move past the incorrect accusation, but Brianna didn't think their burgeoning friendship would survive another finger-pointing episode.

Chapter 6

The day of the promised work party arrived. After Brianna completed a quick yoga routine—she'd started the habit a month ago to gain flexibility and was now helped by Paprika, who liked to clamber over her while she stretched like she was a giant cat tree—she stepped out of her float home armed with work clothes and a hammer, ready to meet whatever task was required of her. Fluffy clouds whipped across the sky in a frenzy of motion, and Brianna was glad she'd had the foresight to put her curly hair in a ponytail to protect it against the wind. There were few things more frustrating than dealing with hair in the eyes.

Clouds kept covering the autumnal sun, and Brianna blinked at the frequent dimming of the light. She squinted toward the sound of voices and followed them until a cluster of float homeowners materialized.

They stood in front of a tiny building between a brilliant green float home and one that looked like a replica of a log cabin with whirligigs stuck into rooftop planter boxes. Lichen covered the roof of the floating building, and a few of the cedar shakes had fallen away. Two men were on the roof examining the damage while five more people milled about and chatted on the dock.

"Brianna," Alicia greeted her when she drew near. Brianna noted with an internal nod that a tight braid held back the other woman's red curls, and the wind didn't move a single strand. "So glad you could make it. We'll be starting as soon as Landon doles out jobs for us. In the meantime, let me introduce you to the others."

Brianna followed Alicia and shook hands with the people she introduced her to. Landon Williams, a rotund middle-aged man with flyaway hair, and his wife Flora, a sapling-thin woman with a toothy grin whom Brianna recognized from the pharmacy, lived in the lime-green house next to the storage building. Fletcher Aarens, who owned a bakery in town, lived with his young son Blake in a float home at the end of the dock. A young woman wearing overalls named Moira Murdock waved at Brianna from a table with pizza boxes on it.

"And that's Corinne Bletchley." Alicia pointed at a petite woman with elfin features and a shock of curly blond hair in a halo around her head that waved in the stiff breeze.

As Alicia finished her introductions, two men descended from the roof. One of them was Alicia's husband Cliff. He took off his glasses to wipe his gleaming forehead.

Alicia smiled at him and then turned back to Brianna. "Looks like we're ready. Let's find out what we can do to help."

Brianna ended up kneeling by a box of asphalt shingles with Corinne and Alicia, counting them into piles for the roofing team. Talk between Alicia and Corinne turned to the recent murder.

"Can you believe it?" Alicia shook her head. "In

sweet little Snuggler's Cove. It hardly bears thinking about. And such a gruesome end."

"It's terrible," Corinne agreed. She wore a pair of patched overalls with a badge that read World's Best Mom. She glanced around and then said in a lower voice, "But you won't catch me crying over it."

Brianna's ears perked up. What was this? Bad blood between yet another person and the sour vineyard owner? It seemed like Sebastian Merle had had his share of opponents. Brianna had her investigative work cut out for her.

"No love lost between you two?" Brianna passed Alicia a shingle and tried not to look too interested. If she was going to help Troy, she needed to dig up as much information as she could manage.

"You could say that." Corinne made a huffing sound and opened a new box of shingles with a utility knife. "He was my landlord."

"Ah, that can be a sticky relationship." Brianna nodded in commiseration. "Did he not keep up your float home well enough?"

"It was more than that, although he wasn't the best at upkeep, no. Stingy guy." Corinne scowled, and Alicia threw her a sympathetic glance, although she kept quiet and continued to place shingles into piles. "When I first started renting the float home," Corinne continued, "it was from Sebastian's old uncle. Sweet guy. We agreed that if he ever wanted to sell the float home, I'd get first dibs as a buyer, and a portion of my rent payments over the years would go toward buying him out."

"Like a rent-to-own?" Brianna asked.

"Something like that. I'm living paycheck to paycheck most months—being a single mom is no cakewalk—and there's no way I can afford the down payment on a house, even one of these float homes. But if my previous rent would help cover it? That, I could swing." Corinne ripped open her box of shingles with a vicious tearing of tape. "But then Sebastian took over his uncle's estate—poor old guy had dementia and lived in a home on the mainland until he passed—which bundled me into it. Now Sebastian wants to sell the float home, and he refuses to honor his uncle's agreement."

"Can't you get a lawyer involved?" Brianna asked. "I'm pretty sure some of them work on a sliding scale."

Alicia shook her head in sympathy, and Corinne answered, "It was a verbal agreement, as Sebastian was quick to point out. I have nothing in writing. Sebastian knew about the deal, but since he denied it and his uncle wasn't well enough to confirm it reliably, I'm stuck up the creek without a paddle." She shrugged tightly. "I'll have to find a new rental."

"I'll help," Alicia said firmly. "You know that. What's the point of knowing a realtor if you can't get some insight into the housing market?"

"I shouldn't have been surprised." Corrine straightened up and handed a shingle from one of Alicia's piles to Cliff when he approached them. "This isn't the first time Sebastian showed his true colors. I heard he helped fund the mini mart at the south end of the island. When the owner didn't do as well as expected—but come on, there are highs and lows in any business—Sebastian pulled his funding without warning. He just wanted to make a buck without thinking of anyone but himself."

"I hadn't heard that," Alicia said. "How terrible."

"He was horrible all over. My friend Drusilla can tell you more stories. She's the owner of Duchess Row, that fruit winery at the north end. He treated her like a second-class citizen all the time." Corrine shook her head. "You can see why I'm not planning to cry at his funeral."

With the shingles unpacked, Alicia moved to grab the cedar shakes that her husband was passing down from the old roof. Corinne walked over to the tins of paint on the dock. Brianna followed her and began opening packages of paintbrushes in preparation for painting the storage shed.

"It's funny to think of murder happening in this little town," Brianna said with a contrived shudder. "I was baking in my café at the time, not a care in the world."

"Yeah, I was at work, too." Corinne pried a paint tin open and stuck a stir stick inside. "With no idea what was happening."

"Where do you work?" Brianna was slightly disappointed that her current suspect might have an alibi, but also relieved that this woman she'd been getting to know—and a neighbor, to boot—likely wasn't the culprit.

"I'm a postie. Mainly package deliveries, so I'm in my van driving around a lot. It's a good gig. I like getting out and about, fresh air, all that."

Brianna grimaced when Corinne wasn't looking.

Driving around by herself wasn't an airtight alibi at all. It would have been easy to drop by Orca Vineyards on her rounds. Corinne had a definite motive and no good alibi, so Brianna couldn't strike her off the suspect list just yet.

"Are you guys still working?" Alicia's teenage son Joel sauntered down the dock with his hands in his pockets. His wide-nosed, impish face grinned at the group. "I thought for sure you'd be done by now."

"Many hands make light work," Alicia quoted at him. "Get up there and help your father, you lazy boy. There's pizza in it for you."

Joel sighed dramatically, but he shimmied up the ladder without another word to his mother. The promise of pizza must have been incentive enough.

"Feeding a teenager is a full-time job sometimes." Alicia laughed. "But I'm pretty good at it. Brianna, would you like to come for dinner at our place sometime? The summer was crazy busy, but now that autumn is here, it would be nice to get together more often with our neighbors."

"I'd love that." Brianna smiled back. She tried to remember a time when she'd regretted moving to Driftwood Island from the big city of Vancouver on the mainland, but she couldn't think of any. If only she didn't have to investigate another murder.

Brianna went back to the café to take over for Oaklyn, who covered Saturday afternoons after Teri's morning shift ended. It was a beautiful sunny day, though, and if Oaklyn wanted to do something fun, Brianna could give her the opportunity. Brianna had already cuddled with Paprika after the work party, and she was ready to take over the till. She had plenty to prepare for her wine and cheese event, and when customers were slow, she could do paperwork.

She pedaled around the bay, weaving around parking cars and slowing for pedestrians. An ice cream vendor with a striped umbrella along the bayside was doing steady business despite the season. This stretch of fine weather had everyone thinking that summer was still here, even though pumpkins were cropping up in the autumnal displays of store windows.

She waved at Hilda Button tottering on the sidewalk, her large handbag firmly on her shoulder—the woman seemed to spend her entire day collecting news in town with the zeal of a gossip column writer—and pulled into the alley beside her café. Once she'd locked up her bike, she entered the kitchen through the side door.

Oaklyn's back was visible through the open doorway, and Brianna snuck into the area behind the counter. Only a few tables were full in the post-lunch lull, and a quiet murmur of chatter suffused the café with a dreamy quality.

"Want a break?" she said quietly.

Oaklyn jumped then turned to glare at her. "You scared me," she accused.

"Sorry. I'm here for the rest of the afternoon if you'd like to take off early. It's a gorgeous day."

Oaklyn's eyes darted around the dining room. "I'm

waiting for someone, actually. I don't mind working a little longer."

Curiosity piqued, Brianna asked, "Is a friend planning on stopping by?"

"It's Rob," Oaklyn said without looking at her. "We might go get ice cream. If he has time today. He said he might stop by."

Brianna bit her lip. This boy was jerking Oaklyn's chain, she was certain of it. What Rob was saying, if she read the subtext correctly, was that he might stop by if he were bored and didn't have anyone better to hang out with. Brianna's heart squeezed tight at Oaklyn's situation. How could she help?

"You're welcome to stay," she said gently, "but why don't you text him to see if he'll be free this afternoon? That way, if he's not, you don't have to hang around waiting for something that might not happen."

That was as close as Brianna dared to calling Rob a liar. Oaklyn scrunched her nose.

"I don't want to seem too eager," she said.

A customer approached, her gold-rimmed glasses gleaming under the counter's lighting, and Brianna let Oaklyn take the order from the lady. Once Oaklyn had poured the tea and delivered a croissant, Brianna continued their conversation.

"It's not eager," she said, "you know, texting Rob to ask if he's coming by. It's showing him that you have a life, too. Let him know that you have other plans you want to make, so if he wants to hang out, he'd better grab his chance."

Oaklyn squinted at her, skepticism rolling off her in

waves. "But what if he decides I seem too busy, and that puts him off?"

Brianna sighed. "It's up to you. But usually, it's more exciting to think that the person you're pursuing isn't waiting with bated breath for you to call."

Oaklyn shrugged and moved to clean the espresso machine. Brianna wandered into the kitchen, but not before she saw Oaklyn sneak her phone out of her pocket and start typing. Brianna smiled. She washed her hands in the back sink and then grabbed a mixing bowl and started to mix dough for a batch of crackers. She'd found the handmade crispy treats were immensely popular in the afternoons.

A few minutes later, Oaklyn slunk into the kitchen. "Maybe I will go, if it's still okay with you," she said with an air of dejection. "I'll see what my friend Stacey is doing today."

"No Rob?" Brianna asked, measuring flour into a bowl.

"He can't make it today. Hopefully, next week."

Brianna nodded and didn't comment further. Clearly, Rob had made other plans for the sunny September day, and Oaklyn wasn't in them. Brianna hoped the girl would see Rob for the liar he was, but she didn't have high hopes, not before he squashed her dreams. It was so much easier to see what was happening from the viewpoint of distance and experience.

Chapter 7

The café needed coins in the cash register. So, before Oaklyn left for the day, Brianna walked briskly to the bank two streets over. Somehow, the three people ahead of her took forever to process, but she eventually reached the front counter and received her rolls of coins.

She smiled at the pile of pumpkins beside the door and whistled as she exited the bank. It was well past time to decorate the café. Pumpkins and scarecrows and falling leaves called to her. Maybe she should try out a pumpkin cheesecake on the café crowd. She'd made one with candied pecans that was delicious. She had the recipe tucked away somewhere…

"Brianna." Esme Alonso's rich voice traveled on the breeze to her ears, and she turned to greet the Gourmand Society member. Esme looked resplendent in an orange silk blouse, fitted black trousers, and huge gold hoop earrings.

"Esme, hi. You look well."

"I do what I can." Esme chuckled and adjusted a wooden bowl that she'd tucked under her arm. "What a tremendous fall day. How are your event plans coming along?"

"Well, thanks." Brianna mentally kicked herself for slacking on the planning front. Investigating the murder had started to take over her waking thoughts. Troy needed her help, after all.

But she couldn't neglect her business along the way.

"I had some thoughts about that." Esme tucked her hand in Brianna's arm and gently steered her in the café's direction. "What if you had a tasting area for all the local cheeses, like a cheese bar of sorts? You could even have the equivalent of a sommelier behind the counter, but for cheese. In fact, you could have two tables, one for cheese and one for wine. It would be a marvelous talking point for the evening, and a great way to break the ice."

"I don't know—"

"You wouldn't have to worry about a thing," Esme promised. "Quentin and I would take care of everything. I know you have a lot on your plate. You focus on those other tasks and leave this one to me. No need to thank me."

Brianna hadn't been planning on thanking Esme. In fact, she wasn't at all keen on Esme's idea and wanted more time to think about it.

But if it kept the other woman busy and out of her hair, Brianna could wait a day or two to put the kibosh on the plan. She had other things on her mind, like ascertaining whether Esme was a killer. Brianna was almost certain the answer was no, but it couldn't hurt to prod a little—carefully, of course, since Brianna didn't want Esme to realize she suspected her.

"Won't you have a lot to do besides my event?" Brianna asked. "I heard you're a judge in the wine competition coming up. That will eat up much of your time. And my event is that same evening."

Esme waved her hand airily as she sidestepped a woman with a stroller who had stopped to deal with her crying baby. "The competition is during the day, and I don't have to do much for it. I can handle both, no problem. I've been a judge for the competition for years, now, although this is the first time Driftwood Island is hosting."

"Who do you expect will enter the competition?" Brianna asked. The more information she could wheedle out of Esme, the better. She didn't know what she was looking for, so every bit helped.

"Wineries from all over British Columbia will enter," Esme replied, "but they always have a special competition for the local contingent. I know your Troy Winchester will be entering for the first time this year with his Whimsical Wines—"

"He's not my Troy," Brianna said with a blush. Things with Troy were going well, but she didn't want to jinx what they had or presume too much. She grimaced at herself sounding as anxious as Oaklyn.

Esme winked at her. "Well on his way to being so. Drusilla Silverleaf of Duchess Row is also planning to enter, I believe. It's a little odd, given how she makes her wines from fruit instead of grapes. The committee is currently discussing how to judge her bottles. And of course, Orca Vineyards always puts on a good show." Esme frowned. "I wonder if they'll still enter. Sebastian was the instigator for everything at his business. He kept a firm hand on the reins. I'm not sure they'll be organized enough to put up a showing this year."

"It's a tight turnaround," Brianna agreed. "Depends

on whether his employees have any knowledge or autonomy. When you're judging, do you know which wine is which?"

"Goodness me, no. It's all anonymous. I am blindfolded justice herself. The competition is cutthroat, and everyone is trying to get ahead and win the medals. It would be too easy to be swayed if I knew which wine to choose."

Esme steered them around a corner and along the main stretch. A few boats dotted the bay at their mooring lines, gleaming white in the autumn sunlight. The Golden Moon's yellow awning beckoned in the distance, and Brianna's heart squeezed at the sight, as it always did.

She didn't have long to get answers out of Esme, so Brianna poured on the coals, trying the same tactic she had used with Corinne.

"I hope Orca Vineyards figures it out," Brianna said with an expression of concern. "It feels unfair that they wouldn't get to enter because Sebastian Merle is dead. What a tragedy. And to think I was merrily baking scones that morning, not a care in the world, while someone was being murdered."

"Are you asking me where I was at the time?" Esme said shrewdly. "You've got a very suspicious nature."

"No, I—"

"It's fine." She waved away Brianna's protests. "I'm happy to rule myself out. I was doing a spot of naked sunbathing in my backyard. Tan lines are the enemy, so I was taking advantage of the last of our warmth and sun."

As far as alibis went, it was weak—Esme hadn't said that anyone was with her—but Brianna had no intention of trespassing on Esme's cordiality any longer. Brianna ignored the notion of Esme's hobby, although she wondered what her neighbors thought of it.

"Why do you care who murdered Sebastian Merle?" Esme asked. She narrowed her eyes at Brianna, then snapped her fingers. "Troy. Are you worried he's a suspect?"

"He is one," Brianna admitted. "And his alibi isn't good. I'm trying to figure out if there's a better culprit to show to the police."

"Fingers are pointing in his direction, that's for sure. I don't know him well enough to say either way, but killing the competition seems extreme. Nobody liked Sebastian, but I don't know who has motive enough to kill him. No one except Quentin, maybe."

"Quentin?" Brianna stopped in front of the Golden Moon and turned to Esme with a searching glance. Esme released her arm and shaded her eyes against the sun.

"Oh, didn't you know? He's Sebastian's nephew. As far as I know, he stands to inherit everything. Their relationship wasn't warm and fuzzy, that's for sure, but Sebastian had no kids, and he would be the last person to donate to a charity. Quentin's the beneficiary, I'm almost certain."

"It's hard to imagine him getting riled up enough to murder someone." Brianna thought about the quiet man with fastidious fashion sense. "But I suppose everyone has their breaking point."

"I'd hate to think it was him. I've known the man for years now, and he's been nothing but kind to me." Esme checked her watch. "Speaking of Quentin, I need to drop off this salad bowl that I borrowed from his place today. I should get moving if I want to do it before my virtual meeting with my editor."

"I can drop it off," Brianna quickly offered. It would be an ideal chance to chat to Quentin about the inheritance. Brianna found it hard to imagine the quiet, mild-mannered society member braining Sebastian with a sharp corkscrew, but the most unassuming cheese could still pack a pungent flavor. "I'm heading that way."

"If you're sure," Esme said, handing the large wooden bowl over with a smile, "I won't say no."

Brianna tucked the bowl under her arm and said goodbye to Esme. While she wasn't a prime suspect— her motivations were weak to nonexistent—she'd given Brianna an excellent lead. Quentin had some explaining to do.

Brianna had a few more things to prepare before she could close the café and visit Quentin, so after chatting for a minute with an exuberant customer gesticulating with his blueberry cream cheese scone in the quiet dining room, she set Esme's bowl aside and pulled on her apron. Once a pan of pull-apart ham and cheese rolls was set to rise slowly overnight under a clean towel in the fridge and the dry ingredients for a large batch of oversized beet muffins destined for mascarpone icing rested in a mixing bowl on the counter, Brianna washed her hands and wandered into the dining room.

"That's not the right way at all," Magnus Pickleton's distinctive gruff voice carried through the room. Brianna zeroed in on the older man seated with Hilda Button. Her needle was flashing as always. Today's sock was a vibrant teal with gold edging. Magnus's bushy eyebrows bunched together menacingly over his mug of coffee. Hilda tsked at him.

"You'll see," she said firmly. "It's the best. Magnus, dear, you have many good ideas, but party planning isn't your strong suit."

"I organized a summer barbecue at the marina last year," he blustered.

"And little Faye fell into the drink and had to be fished out with a net," Hilda reminded him patiently. "Leave it with me. I'll give you your tasks when it's time, don't worry."

Brianna wandered closer to say hello to the pair.

"What party are you planning?" she asked. Was it rude to inquire? In Vancouver, she wouldn't have dreamed of intruding on a discussion of a party without being invited lest it look like she was angling for an invitation. But this was Snuggler's Cove, gossip was currency, and everyone knew everyone else's business. It felt natural to ask.

"Why, your party, my dear." Hilda beamed up at her, her needle flashing. "Your wine and cheese event. We're planning an extra special component."

"And what might that be?"

"Don't you fret." Hilda nodded with a pleased smile on her face. "We have it all handled. No extra stress on your part."

Brianna tried not to let her annoyance show on her face. The Gourmand Society's help with her event was quickly turning from aid into interference. Brianna had a vision for the wine and cheese evening, and it didn't include surprises she hadn't accounted for.

"I won't fret," she said. She wanted to say, "Call it off," but she didn't have the guts to stand up to the group. Magnus she could deal with, despite his bark, but Brianna couldn't imagine defying sweet Hilda. "But let me know what you're planning."

"Oh, it's a secret, my dear. A wonderful surprise."

Brianna gritted her teeth. She hated secrets. Greg had had far too many of them, and it had left an unpleasant taste in her mouth for surprises.

"I'd love to know, when you're ready to talk," she forced out. "Surprises aren't my favorite."

"You'll like this one," Hilda promised. "Oh, I clean forgot. Did you hear, someone dropped off evidence at the Mountie detachment last night? Which is a good thing since they couldn't find any fingerprints on the corkscrew. Anyway, the Mounties found some new evidence this morning. Guess what it was?"

Hilda stared at Brianna expectantly. Brianna shook her head in bewilderment, and Magnus sighed.

"There's no way she could ever guess," he grumbled. "Just tell her."

"Someone who works at Orca dropped off a memory stick," she said in triumph. "You know, one of those computer plug thingies you put files on. They'd finally accessed the security footage from Orca Vineyards at the time of the murder. According to Patty, Sebastian had locked up the access room."

"What did it show?" Brianna leaned forward, eager to hear. Would this crack the case wide open? But why would someone steal the footage only to give it back to the police?

"Troy Winchester was there," Hilda whispered, "just as he'd said he was. But there was also another figure creeping around in the shadows. The person was wearing a hood, Patty said, so they can't tell who it was, but the timing is right." Hilda leaned back and resumed darning her sock. "What do you think about that?"

Brianna blinked at this new information. Another person was skulking around the winery at the time of the murder. But who? And why keep the footage hidden until now?

When her customers finally finished their tea and treats, Brianna closed the café and hopped on her bicycle. She'd never been to Quentin Flagstaff's home, but Esme had described the way clearly enough. A stiff breeze off the water chilled her skin as she rode around Snuggler's Cove, despite the dappled sunshine from racing clouds above.

She turned onto a main road that would take her to Quentin's. Traffic was light today. When a car slowed alongside her, she glanced at it.

Devon Moore peered at her from his cruiser with a grin. "Hi, Brianna. Nice day for a bike ride."

Brianna slowed her pedaling so she wouldn't seem out of breath.

"It's always a nice day for a bike ride when it's your only form of transportation," she said, attempting a breezy tone despite her lack of oxygen.

"Where are you headed? Can I offer you a ride somewhere?"

Wasn't he on the clock? Surely he had more important things to do than to taxi her around.

"That's a kind offer, but I'm close to my destination." Brianna waffled for a minute about what to tell Devon, then decided on the truth. The great thing about always telling the truth was that she didn't have to remember her stories. "I'm stopping by Quentin Flagstaff's house."

Devon's eyes narrowed. "What takes you there? You're not investigating Sebastian Merle's murder, are you?"

"Quentin and I are both in the Gourmand Society," she said with dignity, deftly avoiding a direct answer. "And Esme Alonso asked me to drop off a salad bowl she borrowed from him. See?" Brianna pointed at the bowl in the basket behind her. "There it is."

"All right." Devon glanced suspiciously at the bowl, then shrugged. "Well, if I can't give you a ride, I should let you get on with your day. Take care of yourself."

With that, he accelerated and rolled around the next corner. When his vehicle disappeared behind trees along the side of the road, Brianna bit her lip and pedaled harder. It was easy for Devon to tell her not to investigate. He had the task of supporting the detectives on the case. She could do nothing to help Troy unless she took matters into her own hands. And she was never one to sit idly by when she could help.

Chapter 8

A subdivision on the southeast side of Snuggler's Cove housed many townsfolk, including Macy and Quentin. Lots with detached homes and duplexes filled neighborhood streets with life, and sweeping maples lit with brilliant reds and oranges lined the roads.

Brianna checked the house numbers until she arrived at the correct one. A hanging pottery jug swayed on a wooden pole with the number on it. It was an odd décor choice, but Brianna had grown used to expecting the unexpected on Driftwood Island.

The house was a small rancher with white stucco siding and lime-green curtains in the windows. A short gravel driveway housed a small silver van with rusty wheel wells next to a patch of lawn. Blousy, late-summer chrysanthemums, dahlias, and sunflowers in a riot of bright colors had almost overtaken the dry grass along the edges.

Brianna parked her bike on the gravel then stepped up to the cherry red front door. She paused for a moment, searching for a doorbell. Once she realized there was none, she rapped sharply on the door.

"We're in the backyard," a voice called from around the corner of the house. Brianna followed the sound along flagstones that wandered past glossy green azaleas ringing the rancher. They pulled her through a wooden arch covered with a clematis that was losing its leaves in the chill nights of autumn. Someone in the house was clearly a gardener.

"Brianna." Quentin stared at her from his spot on the small lawn behind the house. He looked odd without his bowtie and with the top button of his shirt open, but he'd carefully slicked his hair to the side and his glasses winked in the sun. "What are you doing here?"

"That's no way to greet a visitor," the man next to him chided. His ebony skin gleamed brown in the light, and his voice held the trace of an accent. "Really, Tintin."

Brianna bit her lip to avoid chuckling at the man's nickname for Quentin.

"I'm here to drop this off." She held out the wooden salad bowl. "Esme said you'd be expecting it. She had a call to take, so I offered since I was heading in this direction."

"Right. Of course." Quentin took the bowl and nodded his thanks.

The other man looked between the two then shook his head. "If you won't introduce me, I will." He held out his hand. "I'm Quentin's husband, Obi."

"Brianna West." She shook his hand, marveling at the stark contrast between Obi and Quentin. Obi wore a loose-fitting linen shirt and pants, a tie-dyed bandana held his curly black hair away from his face, and his dark feet were bare. Brianna could imagine him as a free-spirited artist and wasn't surprised to spy a small shed in the back with a pottery wheel visible through the open door. That explained the hanging jug out front. She continued, "Quentin and I are both members of the Gourmand Society. I'm the owner of the Golden Moon."

"I've tasted your baking a few times when people bring it over. I haven't had the pleasure of visiting your establishment yet, but when I make it into town, I will."

"Oh, I meant to say." Brianna turned to Quentin. "I just heard that Sebastian Merle was your uncle. I'm so sorry for your loss."

"Thanks," Quentin said while Obi snorted softly. "I appreciate that."

With a glance at Obi, Brianna said, "Were the two of you close? Did you visit him much?"

"Close." Obi laughed outright at that. "That's not the word I would use to describe their relationship." When Quentin threw him an exasperated look, he shrugged. "Come on. You know it's true."

Quentin sighed and rubbed his forehead between his glasses and carefully styled hair. "We weren't on the best of terms, although I tried for my mother's sake. She loved the old codger."

"Because she has dementia and remembers Sebastian the way he was as a child," Obi reminded him.

"It will be hard to break the news to her," Quentin said with a shake of his head. "She'll be heartbroken. For a short time, at least. That's the one silver lining of dementia. Maybe I won't tell her, just pretend Sebastian isn't visiting any longer. That might be kinder."

"So you didn't visit Sebastian often, I take it." At Quentin's agreement, Brianna said, "I wonder who the last person was to see him. He sounds like a rather prickly character. Did he have friends or—"

"Not friends," Quentin said quickly. "Not that I knew about, anyway. Maybe someone business-related came by. I didn't see him that morning. I was getting a late breakfast at the Bumblebee."

Quentin gave a half-glance at Obi as he spoke, although the other man was examining the leaves of a nearby shrub and didn't notice. Brianna narrowed her eyes. She smelled a lie in Quentin's words, but she couldn't decide which ones.

"They serve a nice breakfast," she said instead. "I hope Sebastian's death doesn't remain a mystery for long. If Sebastian didn't have any friends or children, do you know what's happening with the winery?"

"I guess that's me," Quentin said. "Once the dust settles and the executor deals with all the paperwork. I have no idea what to do with it, though."

"Just hire the manager to take over operations," Obi said. He wandered over to a bench and grabbed a pair of garden shears. With a nod of satisfaction, he started snipping dying flowers off a climbing rose nearby.

"Maybe." Quentin sighed. "That sounds like more hassle than it's worth, though. I might sell the business. Whatever is easier. We don't need the money."

Brianna thought of the small house and rusting van sitting in its driveway. Was Quentin lying, or were they content with what they had? It was an enviable position, if so.

"I'm sure both options would work out well," Brianna said.

Quentin crossed his arms and gazed at Obi, who had

moved onto another rose bush covered in ripening rosehips. "I hope they find the killer soon. It's distressing to think of a murderer walking around town unchecked. And the police were here earlier, asking questions. It's an altogether uncomfortable situation. I understand they need to follow all possible leads, and since I'm the heir, it was inevitable they'd pay me a visit."

"Hold this for me, Tintin," Obi called out. "I dropped my shears in the bush."

Quentin stepped toward Obi and grabbed the branch he held out to him. The next instant, he leaped back and cursed, shaking his hand vigorously.

"I hate roses," he hissed. "I don't care how pretty they are. We should tear them all up."

"It's just a little thorn prick." Obi frowned at Quentin. "Honestly. Don't overreact."

"I need gloves before I help again." Quentin stalked back to Brianna with a scowl.

Quentin's outburst surprised Brianna. He normally seemed so calm and collected. But maybe that was the problem. Keeping it together for too long led to inevitable blow-ups. Steam had to be released somewhere. Had Sebastian simply been in the wrong place at the wrong time when Quentin exploded?

Quentin resumed their conversation. "But honestly, if I were in the police's shoes, I'd look more closely at Drusilla Silverleaf from Duchess Row."

"You're not the first person to mention her," Brianna said.

Quentin looked at her sharply. His glasses winked in

the sun and made it hard for Brianna to see his eyes. The lack of visual signals was disconcerting.

"She's incredibly competitive and has a chip on her shoulder," he said.

"Not to mention an abrasive personality," Obi called out. He was on his stomach, wriggling under the rose bush to fetch his shears. "And that's saying something, given that I knew your uncle."

"So, she might have a motive?" Brianna's head whirled with new information. It looked like she needed to pay this Drusilla a visit sooner rather than later. Luckily, she had a built-in excuse with her wine and cheese event.

"She would be the first person I'd investigate, if I were the police," Quentin said. "That's all I'm saying."

Brianna left a few minutes later after saying her goodbyes. She had a lot to think about, and she needed to bounce her ideas off someone. It was time to visit Macy.

Macy was out of town Sunday, shopping for clothes with Oaklyn in a town on the larger Victoria Island. While Brianna waited, she did her daily baking for the café then spent the rest of the day working on plans for her event, which included setting up advertisements and getting the schedule sorted down to the last detail.

Macy had an early lunchtime on Mondays at the preschool since the staff took turns helping the little ones with their lunches. Brianna pedaled to the Happy

Hearts building and leaned her bike against the mural filled with sunflowers, squirrels, and butterflies. Chattering children's voices interspersed with the deeper tones of the educators drifted from a window, open in the warmth of the sunny autumn day.

A crisp leaf floated from a maple planted on the boulevard and landed in Brianna's bike basket. She picked it up and twirled it around in her fingers, considering what to tell Macy about her findings so far.

Her friend finally pushed the glass door open. She reached toward the sky in a stretch, her satisfaction showing on her face. "Oh, this morning was busy," she said with a groan. "The munchkins were a handful. Something in the air, maybe. Is it a full moon? It's lucky they're cute."

"Maybe they're worked up from the crisp fall air," Brianna suggested. "Or maybe someone's been sneaking them sugar."

"Can you imagine?" Macy shuddered. "The day after Halloween is always a nightmare, especially when parents put candy into their kids' lunch kits. Anyway, what's up? Not that I don't like to see you for no reason—I'm always happy to shoot the breeze with you—but you have that look in your eye."

"What look?"

"The one that shows you're thinking hard, that you have something to tell me."

"I didn't realize I was that obvious." Brianna pulled on Macy's arm, and they sat on a bench against the wall facing the road. A pickup truck roared by, but otherwise the street was quiet.

"Spill," Macy said with an expectant air. She rummaged in her bag and extracted a thermos and a fork. "Well, spill while I eat. I'm starving, but I can multitask."

While Macy unscrewed her thermos and popped tortellini in her mouth, Brianna spoke.

"I'm investigating Sebastian Merle's murder. You know, Orca Vineyards' owner. They found him floating in a fermentation vat with a head wound last week. You must have heard of it."

"The talk of the town? Hard to escape it." Macy shivered. "What a nasty way to go. All the parents want to talk about it, but we can't say much in front of the kiddos, so it's all winks and whispers and speaking in code. If the kids learn about it, half of them will be awake all naptime from nightmares, and the other half will do reenactments with playdough." Macy frowned. "But why are you looking into it? I know you solved your aunt's case a few months back, but are you still trying your hand at detective work, just for fun?"

"Not exactly. I wouldn't mind leaving the investigation for the police to handle, but they seem to have very few clues to work with." Brianna crossed her legs and leaned back. "The problem is, they have Troy under the microscope, and it doesn't look great for him. I'm trying to get him off the hook and get the detectives on the path toward finding the actual killer."

"Troy, hey? Why do they think he's the one?"

"Business competitor, mainly. Oh, and he was seen leaving Orca Vineyards that morning. He might have been the last one to see Sebastian alive. Before the murder, that is."

Macy tilted her head at Brianna. "And you're sure Troy isn't the killer? I know that's a terrible thing to say, but…"

"It's worth considering, I know." Brianna shook her head vigorously. "I'm positive, and I don't think that's me being naïve. He was the first one to tell me he was at Orca that morning, and he even confessed that he and Sebastian had argued. Why would a murderer admit to that? And I've known him for a bit, now, and he's very caring. I just can't see it, you know?"

"That's true."

"And there's security footage of another person at the winery at the time of the murder, so it was probably them. I just wish the person hadn't been skulking in the shadows wearing a hoodie. They can't even tell if it's a man or a woman."

Macy drummed her fingers on her knees, then took another bite of her tortellini. "So, we've ruled Troy out," she said through a mouthful. She swallowed. "Who else wanted Sebastian dead?"

"It sounds like there was a lineup," Brianna admitted. "He wasn't a well-liked citizen of Driftwood Island. But I have a few leads. Corinne Bletchley—she's another float home resident—she had some bad dealings with Sebastian over her rental property. He was about to toss her and her son onto the street before he died. She could barely keep her rage contained when she told me about it, even though he was already dead."

"Suspicious," Macy said. "And that's a strong motive, wanting to protect your child from homelessness."

"And her alibi is weak. She's a postal worker, so she was on the road alone. It would have been easy to swing past Orca." Brianna held up her hand and checked off her fingers. "That's Corinne. Then there's Esme Alonso and Quentin Flagstaff. Honestly, I don't think Esme is a great candidate. Her motive is weak—she had some bad dealings with Sebastian in the past when she commented on his wines in a food magazine—and although she doesn't have an alibi, since she was sunbathing nude, alone in her backyard at the time—"

"Of course she was." Macy snickered. "If I had half the self-confidence that woman has…"

"I just don't see it," Brianna continued. "I'm not ruling her out yet, but since I falsely accused her last time, I don't want to make the same mistake this time."

"That's fair. What about Quentin Flagstaff? He's in the Gourmand Society, right? I don't know much about him."

"Apparently, he's Sebastian's heir." Brianna raised her eyebrows at a significant look from Macy. "Exactly. Money is always a powerful motive. Quentin said he wasn't interested in the money, but he was also acting shifty. He was lying about something—I'm just not sure what. And he has a bit of a temper, which I hadn't realized before."

"You know, I heard something about Quentin the other day." Macy prodded her pasta with her fork while she gazed across the road in thought. "What was it? He was asking for a loan at the bank, that was it. Wanda at the counter has a voice that could wake up the mountains, it's so loud. No secrets at the bank, that's for sure."

"So, we can call hogwash on his disinterest in money," Brianna said. "I guess he's desperate for it, if he can't wait for his uncle's estate to be settled."

"Whew." Macy leaned back against the bench after finishing her tortellini. "Anyone else?"

"Just one. Drusilla Silverleaf."

"Why does she sound familiar?"

Brianna waited while a pedestrian walked by. The woman's large purse swung from her shoulder, and she touched her curled bob with a self-conscious air.

When she had passed out of hearing, Brianna said, "She owns Duchess Row, that fruit winery on the north end. Apparently, she and Sebastian had bad blood. I haven't spoken to her yet, but she's next on my list."

"It sounds like you have your work cut out for you. Make sure you take someone along when you interview people, okay? I know you. You like to dive into interrogations without thinking about your safety."

"You sound like Devon Moore," Brianna muttered. "Fine, I'll take Dot along when I visit Duchess Row."

"Speaking of Devon, you ought to loop the police in on whatever you find," Macy added. "I know you don't have anything concrete yet, but it's still good information, especially if it goes along with something they've found already."

"I haven't found anything yet, not really," Brianna protested. "They're going to tell me to run along and leave the detective work to them."

"At least tell Devon. He'll hear you out. He did before."

Brianna stared across the road at a playground's slide and swing set that faced them. Devon had pushed back against her suggestions at the start, but he'd eventually listened and had even acknowledged that her findings had been invaluable. Macy was right. Devon wouldn't brush her off. And didn't she owe it to Troy to do everything she could to clear his stained name?

"Okay," she said at last. "I'll talk to him. Changing the topic, what's up with Oaklyn and this Rob fellow? Do you know the story there?"

"She's really into him from what I can glean from her monosyllables." Macy slid her thermos into her bag, then played with the tines of her fork absentmindedly. "I've only seen him once, when I dropped her off at school one day when she was running late. I don't know much about him, otherwise. Why? Has she told you anything?"

"Nothing much," Brianna admitted. "But from the few things she's said, I wonder if he's yanking her chain. He gave her the teenage boy equivalent of 'washing his hair' to get out of a date, and I can't help but wonder if he got a better offer that afternoon, but he still wants to keep Oaklyn around for options." Brianna sighed. "I don't know, maybe I'm reading more into it than is actually happening. I just hate to think that Oaklyn is being lied to. That's a terrible feeling."

"I hope not." Macy twisted the fork in her hands.

"It's just so much easier to see with years of experience behind us. She's so young, and all this dating business is new."

"Can you try to ask her about it?" Macy gazed at Brianna beseechingly. "She won't tell me anything—I'm her mother, and we don't have one of those tell-all sort of relationships, unfortunately—but she might open up to you. You're the cool aunt."

Brianna snorted. "I don't know about that, but I can try."

"Thank you." Macy heaved an enormous sigh. "I hope she's not falling for the wrong guy. Oh well, secrets will out, eventually."

Chapter 9

Brianna rode from Macy's preschool directly to the municipal offices parking lot. She was warmer than she'd expected, and her sweater now lay folded in her basket, unneeded on the warm day.

The Royal Canadian Mounted Police detachment's door was open to encourage a breeze, and Brianna flipped the kickstand of her bike before walking in. The Mountie office looked just like the last time she'd been in here—same three chairs against the window, same linoleum-floored hallway—except for a decorative gourd on the counter that gave a minor concession to the season.

"Excuse me," Brianna said to Lennox, the lanky officer seated behind the desk today. "Is Corporal Moore around?"

"He's in a meeting," he said. "If you have an urgent police matter to discuss with him, I can take your information instead."

"No, no." Brianna backed away. "It wasn't anything important. I'll stop by another time."

She exited the office, her disappointment more pronounced than she'd expected. Before she had time to ponder her reaction, footsteps pounded on the sidewalk behind her. She turned around.

"Brianna," Devon panted. He halted in front of her. "I heard you stopped by. My meeting just finished.

What can I help you with?"

Brianna pushed down her sense of relief at the sight of his face. This case was important to her, and she was glad to give her clues to Devon since he could pass on anything relevant to the detective in charge.

"Yes, thanks." She gathered her thoughts. "I've been asking around about the Sebastian Merle murder."

Devon's brow furrowed, and his lips tightened. "I know you were helpful with your aunt's case, but you really need to let the detectives do their job. They have plenty of leads to work with, and no one has wrongfully confessed to the crime."

"But did you know that Corinne Bletchley is furious that Sebastian reneged on a real estate agreement she'd made with his uncle?" Brianna challenged. "Or that Quentin Flagstaff, Sebastian's heir, might be lying about his alibi and his need for the money promised him? Or that Drusilla Silverleaf was Sebastian's foremost business rival?"

Devon huffed a sigh. "And you've spoken to all these people, have you?"

"Almost all of them. How else was I supposed to get information out of them?"

"Do you remember what happened last time?" he demanded. "How you almost died at the hands of the killer?"

Brianna swallowed. She hadn't forgotten. Sometimes, she still woke in the middle of the night from nightmares.

"But it all worked out. And I can't stand by while a murderer walks free."

After a long pause, Devon said, "I'll pass on your conjectures to the detectives, okay? But keep a low profile. Please. I'm going to go gray, watching you risk yourself like this."

Warmth suffused Brianna's cheeks at the thought of Devon caring about her wellbeing.

"Oh, I almost forgot," he continued. "I smoked some trout yesterday. Are you still interested in trying some? I can drop it off soon."

Oaklyn's comment about kingfishers brought more heat to Brianna's cheeks. She tried to ignore the memory.

"I'd love some."

Their stretch of sunshine had finally broken, and white clouds scuttled across a patchy gray sky. The afternoon wind combed through tree branches and dislodged leaves that tumbled across Dot's gravel driveway. Brianna zipped her windbreaker up to her chin while she waited for her aunt to get ready.

"That ought to do it," Dot said finally. She tossed a wrench toward her front porch in a high arc. The tool thudded on a wooden step, and Zola bleated from the noise. Dot leaned over the bike's trailer, where her goat stood ensconced in her nylon enclosure. "Sorry, my sweet. I didn't mean to scare you. Would you like a bit of my apple?"

"She has you wrapped around her hoof." Brianna laughed at her aunt, who made a face.

"Let me dote on my goat in peace." She unzipped the door and dropped her half-eaten apple inside. Zola pounced on the treat and nibbled it with satisfied crunching.

They wheeled down the gravel driveway and up the long hill that took them through Dot's land and out of the valley. Dot was huffing with exertion by the time they reached the top of the hill, and Brianna stopped on the side of the road to enjoy the view while her aunt recovered. It was stunning, even with the dim skies and winds that threatened to push Brianna backward. Long stretches of green-clad hills rolled into pastures and farmland in the valleys. Steely gray ocean lay beyond them, and it was tinged with a hint of blue. A few brave sailboats drifted in the strait, their sails well-reefed in the strong winds.

"Ready for more?" Brianna asked her aunt, who had finally stopped breathing so heavily.

"Ready for going down," she replied. "I can't believe you convinced me to ride all the way to the north end."

"Zola's weight on the back is what's really throwing you off."

"But how could I leave her when we're going on an adventure?" Dot reached back and scratched Zola's ear through a rip in the trailer, and the goat butted her hand in return. "Besides, you promised me wine at the end of this."

"Then, we'd better get to Duchess Row." Brianna glanced at Dot. "We also have another goal this afternoon. I'm trying to clear Troy's name from this murder business. The owner of Duchess Row was apparently at loggerheads with Sebastian, and I want to question her.”

“You are rather good at investigating,” Dot conceded. “But make sure you don’t end up at the wrong end of a cattle prod this time, okay?”

“The Mounties have already given me the lecture,” Brianna grumbled. “I’ll be careful, I promise. And that’s why you’re with me.”

“Far be it from me to stop a woman indulging her passions. I’m with you all the way, whether you need a distraction for investigating or someone to drink with.” Dot put her foot on her pedal. “Come on, we have wine to taste.”

After a long ride north through winding lanes, thick forest, and open farmland, they reached a carved wooden sign on the road announcing Duchess Row accompanied by a picture of a tiara perched on the first letter. The winery itself was invisible from the road, but a paved driveway wound through a thick stand of conifers. Brianna led the way, with Dot and Zola following on Dot’s ticking bicycle.

Past the firs and cedars, the sky opened to a vista of farmland. Rows of fruit trees stood in orderly lines before a farmhouse with wood siding perched on a foundation of rocks cemented together. The dark-stained house needed repairs, although solar panels covered the mossy roof. Brianna wondered if she should invest in a few panels for her float home. Was winter really that rough on the island? She hadn’t expected extreme weather in the mild coastal climate and said as much to her aunt.

"It's not the weather," Dot said. "Any trees that fall on a power line can knock out the power for days while we wait for the off-island electrical company to fix it. I usually hunker down with a few candles, although I have a generator for dire occasions."

Brianna put solar panels on her mental list of things to research. Maybe once this wine and cheese event was over—and Sebastian's murderer found—she would have a minute to breathe and ponder things like electrical services.

"I wonder what sort of fruit trees Juicy has here," Dot said with interest.

"Juicy?" Brianna stared at her aunt. "Is that what you call Drusilla? Do you know her?"

"Strangely enough, she is my high school friend's stepdaughter." Dot chuckled. "Small world, hey? I guess we had something in common, both moving to this little island in the Pacific."

"Juicy." Brianna snorted. "What a name."

"How could we not call her that, saddled with a name like Drusilla? I wouldn't have pegged her for a vintner, but she's making a name for herself. I've tried her apple cider, and I know she has a kiwi wine as well."

"Let's find out what she's offering." Brianna swung her leg off her bike and flicked the kickstand, but Dot stopped her with a hand.

"Wait, I think I see Juicy in the orchard. Let me get Zola out, then we can go meet her."

Dot unzipped Zola's trailer while Brianna squinted through the greenery to spot whoever Dot had seen.

Once Dot fitted the goat with a leash of twine, she tugged Zola forward, and the three of them walked into the grove of fruit trees.

Apples dripped off the branches, and overripe ones fell onto the grass, where curious insects wandered over them. Some apples were a brilliant red, some were greenish-yellow, and still others were pale green, shot with streaks of rose. A wheelbarrow half-filled with fruit waited beside a ladder.

A row over, plump pears dangled from trees, waiting for their turn to be picked. Leafy trees occupied the row, and Brianna guessed that whatever variety they were, someone had already harvested them.

Brianna finally caught sight of Drusilla between the apples and pears, and she ducked between two apple trees to reach the row. Drusilla contemplated a pear, turning it around in her hand for inspection. Her thin brown hair hung lank around her narrow face, made even thinner by a pair of oversized, black-framed glasses. Her mouth was narrow and drawn, and she appeared either dehydrated or as if she'd recently sucked a lemon. Brianna shook her head to clear it of the unworthy thought, but it remained in her mind and forced her to control her smile.

"Juicy," Dot called out in a hearty voice. "How are you? It's Dot Dubois, here with my niece Brianna West. Long time, no see."

Drusilla looked up, and her face grew even more pinched. Brianna hadn't realized it was possible without the woman imploding.

"Dot," she said in a pained voice. "It's been a long

time since anyone has called me that. I usually go by Drusilla now."

"You have a lovely orchard," Brianna said to steer the topic away from contentious nicknames. "What types of fruit do you grow?"

"Apples, pears, plums," Drusilla rattled off, as if eager to impart her knowledge. "And raspberries. I buy my kiwis from another farm on the island. I tried growing cherry trees, but that was a waste of time. Too difficult keeping the birds off the fruit. Ended up making an end table out of the wood."

"I own the Golden Moon, the cheese café in Snuggler's Cove," Brianna said with her hand outstretched. "We're hosting a wine and cheese event on Friday to showcase local artisans. I was hoping to taste a few of your wines to use for the event."

"Oh!" Drusilla was momentarily speechless. "Oh, of course. Come. Follow me to the tasting room. I have some excellent bottles for you to try."

They traipsed through the orchard after Drusilla, Dot occasionally pulling Zola along when she tried to eat apples off the ground. Brianna pocketed a fallen apple to keep Zola occupied while they were tasting the wines.

"How's life treating you, Juicy—I mean, Drusilla?" Dot wrinkled her nose. "It's quite a mouthful," she whispered to Brianna.

"Business is booming," Drusilla said primly. She sidestepped a rake and clucked her tongue. "The pickers are so careless. Leaving tools lying around. What if it rains? Then we'll have rust issues. And they must be taking the longest tea break in the world. I'll have to rustle them out here soon." She checked her watch and sniffed. "I suppose they still have a few minutes. But if they're not out there on time, they'd better watch out. I'm not paying them to loaf around."

"Glad I'm not picking fruit here," Dot muttered to Brianna. "Juicy was always quick to fly off the handle. I'd hate for her to be my boss."

They approached a low, narrow building. One end was almost entirely glass-sided, with a wooden counter inside and a row of bottles behind it. The rest of the building was windowless. Brianna guessed that processing and fermentation happened on that end.

Drusilla opened the glass door for them to enter, although she gave Dot a stern look when she tried to bring Zola inside. With inaudible grumbling, Dot tied the goat to a fence post, and Brianna gave the animal her apple to keep her occupied. Once the humans were all inside, Drusilla stepped behind the counter formally. With crisp motions, she pulled out two wine glasses and three bottles from a fridge behind her.

"Let's start with the plum wine," she announced. She tipped a bottle into the first glass, and deep purple liquid sloshed inside. Another splash entered the next glass, and then she pushed the glasses toward the two women. "Please. See what you think."

Brianna sniffed the wine then took a sip of the sweet, aromatic drink.

"Lovely," she said. "I could see that pairing nicely with a nice blue, maybe a Gorgonzola."

"Ooo, quite right, darling." Dot smacked her lips

with pleasure. "Nice one, Ju—Drusilla. What else do you have?"

Deftly, Drusilla uncorked the next bottle. A pale-yellow liquid spun in a whirlpool in Brianna's glass.

"Pear," the proprietor announced. "It's a light, crisp beverage. We'll move onto the dessert wines at the end. That's often when the fruit wines shine their brightest."

Brianna sipped the pale liquid. The flavor was a strange mixture of fruity and dry.

"It's a bit sharp, don't you think?" Dot was never one to hide what she truly thought. Brianna winced when Drusilla puffed up like an angry cat.

"It's not sharp," she hissed. "It's crisp. A finely balanced astringency that is highly prized by those in the know."

Brianna and Dot glanced at each other. Was the other woman always so quick to take offense? It didn't surprise Brianna that Drusilla and Sebastian had been at odds. If the antics Brianna had witnessed at the liquor store were typical of Sebastian, then it was no wonder Quentin had pointed fingers at his competitor. Brianna couldn't imagine them being in the same room without erupting at each other, even without the impetus of being business rivals.

Chapter 10

They tried a few more wines, a dessert raspberry and the greenish-hued kiwi wine, and Dot refrained from making any additional comments that might rile Drusilla up. Brianna chose the plum and kiwi for her event and ordered a case of each, which Drusilla rang through the till with a pleased expression and a promise to deliver the cases in a few days.

"Will you be entering the wine competition this year?" Brianna asked when Drusilla handed her the receipt for her purchase. "It's coming up shortly."

Drusilla scoffed. "Competitions are so vulgar. I don't need the approval of some elitist judges to tell me that my products are superior. My own taste buds and my customers are proof enough."

"I have heard that the medals help boost sales," Brianna said mildly. Drusilla's comment seemed shortsighted, but maybe something else was behind the snobbish words.

"So they say." The vintner sniffed. "Well, maybe, now Sebastian Merle of Orca Vineyards is done and dusted, I might throw in a bottle or two, just for fun."

"Why does it matter if Sebastian is dead?" Dot asked with a curious tilt to her head.

Movement outside caused all three to turn. Zola trotted away, her rope dragging behind her with a frayed end. Had the animal chewed through it?

Dot gave a shout and headed out the door. It slammed shut behind her as she chased Zola's perky white tail through the orchard.

Brianna chuckled then turned to Drusilla. "Sorry about that. You were saying…"

"She'd better catch that goat." Drusilla craned her neck to follow Dot's passage through her trees before she returned her gaze to Brianna. "Sebastian. Right. He was always obnoxiously vocal with his disapproval of Duchess Row. Said I didn't deserve to call my drinks wines since they weren't made from grapes." Drusilla straightened the bottles on the counter into a fussy line. "He bad-mouthed me to all the local restaurants, liquor stores, anyone he could get to listen, really." Drusilla's face reddened, and she put her palms on the counter. "Totally preposterous. Rude, is what it was. Uncalled for, condescending, and unnecessary. Who gave him the right to decide what a wine should be made from? Grapes are just fruit, aren't they?"

She was nearly panting with fury by this point. Brianna took a surreptitious step back from the angry woman. Drusilla had just jumped to first place in her suspect list. She had motives coming out her ears, and a fiery temper to boot.

"So, now you don't have to deal with Sebastian Merle, you might enter the competition?" Brianna steered the conversation gently.

Drusilla took a deep breath, and some of the angry red splotches on her face receded. "That's right. A lucky break. Or at least, a silver lining of a tragedy," she said quickly to cover her callous comment. "Not that I care about medals, but maybe it could be an interesting event, now that the terror Sebastian isn't there to sneer at me."

"I take it you didn't visit Orca Vineyards much." Squeezing suspects for alibis was Brianna's most challenging task, and she had to get inventive with every one—at least, if she didn't want them to feel like they were being interrogated.

"Ha. Certainly not. I would never go there! Sebastian would have run me off the property, no doubt. No, my place is here, among the fruit trees that give me such glorious fruit for my wines. That's where you'll find me, most days. There's something peaceful about this orchard, with its orderly rows and waiting fruit." Drusilla shook her head. "No, I haven't seen Sebastian for weeks, and that was how I liked it."

"I wonder who did see him," Brianna mused aloud to get Drusilla's opinion. "Someone killed him, after all. He must have had visitors."

Dot had finally wrangled Zola, and she appeared between the rows of fruit trees, heading in their direction. She was red-faced with twigs in her graying blond hair, although the little goat trotting next to her on a leash had an immaculate white coat.

"I don't blame whoever it was," the other woman said. "He was a nasty piece of work. I know we're not supposed to speak ill of the dead, but I doubt you'll find anyone who disagrees with me. I wonder who would stoop to care enough about the old grouch to do something like that. Someone else he scorned or maybe someone with a screw loose."

Dot entered the glass tasting room, looking disgruntled. "Crazy creature. I swear she was playing games with me."

Drusilla snapped her fingers. "Hey, what about that crazy guy Bacchus? He's nutty enough to lose his cool and murder someone."

"Bacchus?" Dot let loose a rolling belly laugh. "You think he killed Sebastian?"

"You laugh," Drusilla said darkly. "But he's nuttier than a fruitcake. I could see him snapping. He and Sebastian had history. Sebastian really had it in for him, and that sort of animosity adds up." Drusilla checked her watch. "Is there anything else I can help you with? I have an appointment coming up shortly."

Brianna said her thanks, and she and Dot gathered the unrepentant Zola and wandered back to their bicycles.

"What do you think?" Brianna said under her breath to Dot.

"Do I think Juicy did it?" Dot twisted her mouth in thought. "Honestly, I wouldn't rule it out. I could see her flying off the handle and swinging the closest metal object at someone's head. Nasty temper, that one."

"I agree. But what about this Bacchus character that she mentioned? Is he worth exploring?" Brianna frowned. "Funny name. Isn't that the Roman god of wine or something?"

"God of wine and revelry." Dot chuckled as she coaxed a reluctant Zola into the trailer. With a zip of the enclosure, she threw her leg over the seat of her bike, and the two women pedaled slowly down the driveway. "Bacchus is a character, all right. I would have said he was harmless enough, but with that many bricks short of a load, who knows?"

"Why the name?"

"He fancies himself the reincarnation of Bacchus. His girlfriend styles herself a Maenad, one of the wild women who attend the god. Like I said, totally bonkers. But every year around this time he throws an epic party. If you're ever invited, go. He invited me twice, and I hardly remember what happened."

"I guess that means you had a good time?" Brianna wasn't in the habit of drinking until her memory faded, but she could picture her aunt going that far occasionally.

Dot laughed. "The best. Anyway, he could be worth investigating, but my money's on Juicy. Or Quentin Flagstaff after what you told me. Follow the money, right? He inherited. That's pretty damning evidence, right there."

Brianna chewed over her list of suspects on the ride home. Overall, she agreed with Dot's opinions. Juicy was volatile with a grudge, and Quentin had the most to gain from Sebastian's death.

But she wasn't about to leave any stone unturned. She would pay the mysterious Bacchus a visit.

Brianna's mind was settled about serving wines from the three wineries on Driftwood Island. She'd already purchased from Duchess Row, and she could figure out what to buy from Whimsical Wines the next time she met up with Troy. That left Orca Vineyards.

Juggling her investigation with her wine and cheese event planning wasn't easy, but she asked Macy to find out where Bacchus lived so she could focus on collecting the rest of her wines. The next afternoon, once her baking was done and Teri was cheerily serving post-lunch tea to customers, Brianna wheeled into the driveway of Orca Vineyards to do a final tasting and buying session. She'd tried to call Troy before arriving just to hear his voice, but his phone had clicked over to voicemail. No matter. She would see him soon.

No ambulances or groups of frightened people gathered around Orca Vineyards' converted barn today. Instead, a few workers picked grapes among the vines, and an open sign hung from the door.

Brianna parked her bike and walked into the tasting room. Instead of Duchess Row's overwhelming glass, the designer of this room had chosen a West Coast feel, with a red cedar counter and a glass backsplash that had a sandblasted killer whale jumping across it. Wine bottles were prominently displayed along a wood-paneled wall, and a few bistro tables dotted the edge of the small room. A chattering couple in their sixties occupied one table, but the room was otherwise empty except for a lean man in his early thirties with a mop of floppy curls behind the counter. Brianna vaguely recognized him from her previous visit, when he'd spoken to the woman with a blond braid. He grinned a greeting.

"Afternoon. My name is Mike, and I'm the

sommelier here today. Can I interest you in a sampler of Orca Vineyards' finest?"

"Yes, please." Brianna leaned against the counter. "I'm planning on purchasing a case for my wine and cheese event at the Golden Moon."

"I've seen that place. Any good?" Mike grinned again to show he was joking. "Well, I'd better showcase our best. Here, try these three."

"I must admit, I was surprised to see the tasting room open, what with recent events and all." Brianna picked up the offered glass and swirled it to sniff the wine's aroma.

Mike lowered his voice and leaned toward Brianna. "To tell you the truth," he said conspiratorially, "the old guy didn't have much to do with the day-to-day running of the place. I manage the winery for the most part, and I didn't see any reason we should shut it down. It would be a shame to have all those grapes go to waste, and everyone knows what they need to do. Honestly, it would be more work for me to find homes for all the grapes, not to mention all the payroll paperwork headache if we closed, than to just keep the place running like the well-oiled machine it is."

"I guess that makes sense." Brianna couldn't fault his logic, although she wondered if Mike were a suspect, given his position at the winery. "And what did you think of Sebastian, as an employer?"

Mike shrugged and uncorked a bottle then poured the pale liquid into a clean wine glass. "He was hard-nosed, but we rubbed along okay. He trusted me to get the job done, albeit with plenty of oversight. I'll keep things going for a while here, but I was planning on moving back east soon to be with my girlfriend, so this isn't a long-term gig for me."

No grudges against the victim, no motivation for killing him… Mike wasn't looking likely as a suspect. Still, she had to cover her bases.

"Did you notice anything the morning of the murder?" she asked.

"I wasn't even here," he said. "It was my day off, and I was getting my hair cut that morning. I only came back when they called me about the murder."

That was a good alibi, but Brianna glanced at his overgrown locks with confusion.

He laughed. "You should have seen it before. Down to my shoulders. I don't cut it too short because my girlfriend likes it shaggy."

Brianna sighed and sipped her wine. Mike wasn't the culprit. She'd stick to Quentin and Juicy as her prime suspects. Oh, and Bacchus. He'd twigged her curiosity.

She tasted the wines Mike offered her and decided on two. She placed the order for her event to be delivered shortly. After she'd finished paying, Mike waved at someone outside the window.

"Shelley, there you are," Mike said when a blond woman arrived, her round face recognizable from Brianna's first visit to Orca Vineyards. "Brianna, this is the apprentice vintner Shelley Bins. Shelley, Brianna just ordered a case of wine for her wine and cheese event. Maybe you could show her around the winery?"

"Of course," Shelley declared brightly. "Right this way, Brianna. So nice to meet you."

A little bemused by Shelley's bright-eyed cheer, Brianna followed the other woman out of the tasting room and into the converted barn. Well-sealing doors that opened into a climate-controlled space had replaced the former rolling door. The area smelled faintly of yeast and fruit.

Brianna narrowed her eyes at Shelley's back as she chatted nonstop about the things they were passing, such as large tanks and barrels, lab equipment, and the bottling line. Brianna nodded occasionally and murmured insightful responses like, "mm-hmm," as they walked through the processing room. Meanwhile, she was eyeing Shelley for murderous tendencies.

When Shelley took a breath, Brianna jumped in. "It must have been a shock for everyone when Sebastian Merle died," she said in a concerned voice.

Shelley's face fell. "That's the truth. How unexpected! Well, of course, a murder is almost always unexpected. I don't know who would have done such a thing. It boggles the mind. It's frustrating, too."

"How so?"

"I was this close," she held up her finger and thumb together, "to getting a letter of recommendation from Sebastian. I'm an apprentice vintner, and I'm looking to move to another winery to gain more experience. That letter would have gotten me places, you know? And he was going to give it to me, too. He said he would." She sighed dramatically. "Now I'll have to talk up my own skills instead of relying on a letter. It's too bad." She put a hand to her mouth. "I'm sorry, that sounded so cruel, didn't it? It's also terrible that Sebastian died, of course."

"Did you and he get along?" Brianna asked gently.

"Oh, he was a right curmudgeon," Shelley said cheerfully. "But I know how to handle those. My grandfather was even worse, if you can believe it, and I had plenty of experience dealing with him as a teenager. He lived with us, to my poor mother's chagrin. No, Sebastian didn't bother me like he did others."

"Who do you think he bothered most?" Brianna asked, curious to get Shelley's view on the subject. She couldn't imagine the smiling woman murdering the victim, especially without a smidgen of motivation to back up the act. But as someone who worked closely with Sebastian, her opinion was valuable.

"Who do I think murdered him, you mean?" Shelley raised her eyebrows. "That's a good question. I don't know that I want to be pointing any fingers. It's hard to believe of anyone." She bit her lip.

Brianna leaned forward. Shelley had someone in mind, but she didn't want to say. "I'm not the police," she said gently. "And I'm not a gossip. You don't have to worry about getting anyone into unwanted trouble."

She crossed her fingers behind her back. Brianna didn't have the law on her side and couldn't make any arrests, but she would investigate if Shelley had anything interesting to tell her.

"It's just that crazy guy down on the east side of the island," Shelley said in a rush. "He thinks he's some Roman god reborn. Bacchus, maybe? A total lush and that's from someone who loves wine. I don't know if he knows one end of the bottle from the other half the time. He used to infuriate Sebastian to no end. I gather they were school friends, long ago, and the guy kept pestering Sebastian to sponsor his yearly wine festival." Shelley tittered. "Well, hardly a festival. A drunken slosh-fest, maybe. Sebastian wouldn't hear of it."

"Didn't want to be associated with that sort of thing?" Brianna guessed.

"Exactly. Who would? Orca Vineyards has a reputation to uphold. Anyway, it got so bad that Sebastian wouldn't even sell this guy anything, and he went around to all the liquor stores forbidding them from selling Orca bottles to him." Shelley shook her head. "What a nightmare. Way too much drama for me. Although, I don't see how Bacchus could have killed Sebastian. When he's sober, he's as sweet as a sleepy kitten. When he's drunk, I doubt he has the coordination to pull off a murder."

Brianna huffed out a breath. Bacchus was worth investigating but her money was still on Quentin or Juicy. Their motivations felt so much stronger than some delusional man who wanted wine for his party.

"Anyway, enough of that cheery topic." Shelley beamed at her. "One last room to look at. It's our cellar for aging the wines once they're bottled. That's the last step in their lives here. Once they finish aging, they're ready to be sold and enjoyed."

Shelley pushed open a sturdy wooden door in an interior wall then gasped. Brianna darted forward to see why.

Chapter 11

Recessed lights in the ceiling illuminated the cement floors and metal racks of the wine cellar. Glass twinkled in dangerous shards everywhere, and red wine pooled like blood on the floor, dripping from bottle racks lined against the walls. A small bistro table and two chairs lay overturned in the center of the room, surrounded by spilled wine and glass.

"No." Shelley clutched a hand to her chest. "No, no, no. Thousands of dollars of inventory, gone. Such a waste. Who would do this?"

Brianna's eyes flicked around the room, searching for clues. When she spotted a wine-stained scrap of cloth dangling from the sharp end of a rack, she pointed it out.

"Look," she whispered. "Was that there before, or did the culprit leave it?"

Before Brianna could warn her away, Shelley darted forward and snatched the scrap off the metal edge. Her face grew even paler.

"It's undyed, coarse-woven linen," she choked out. "I'm sure of it."

"What does that mean?"

Shelley whirled toward Brianna, her eyes huge and round in her normally cheerful face.

"I like to sew in my spare time. I know my fabrics and note when I see someone wearing unusual ones.

It's rare to see cloth that isn't dyed. The only person I've seen on the island wearing this sort of fabric is Bacchus."

Brianna stuck around while Shelley called the police and ran back to tell Mike what had happened. The loss of product must have been a major blow—so much hard work from so many people went into those bottles—and Brianna could sympathize with the tears leaking out of Shelley's eyes. She wanted to know what the Mounties would conclude from this sabotage, so she lurked in the background until they arrived.

The timing of the Orca Vineyards' wine sabotage was too close to Sebastian's murder to be coincidental. If the two events weren't related, Brianna would swear off dairy.

For a month, anyway. No point in risking too much.

The police cruiser rolled into Orca Vineyards' parking lot, and Devon and Lennox stepped out of the vehicle. Shelley ran up to greet them.

"It's horrible," she burbled. "Glass and wine everywhere. Such a tragic waste. Thousands of dollars in puddles on the floor. It was totally fine this morning when I checked."

"Show us where the damages are," Devon said gently but firmly, and Shelley led the way to the cellar. Devon jerked his head in surprise when he spotted Brianna, and she gave him a small wave.

"What are you doing here?" he said in an undertone

after letting Lennox take the lead after Shelley. "Why are you always in the thick of things?"

"Total coincidence, I swear." Brianna walked alongside him, curious to see his and Lennox's reaction to the mess. "I was ordering wine for my event, and Shelley gave me a tour after. That's when we found the broken bottles in the cellar."

Devon shook his head but said nothing more. Shelley opened the cellar door and looked away as if unable to witness the destruction again.

Lennox whistled. "That's a right mess," he said. He sidled further into the room and glanced around, careful to avoid stepping in wine or glass. "Any ideas who might have done it?"

"Yes." Shelley pointed with a trembling finger at the scrap of linen she'd hung back on the metal rack. "It's that madman, Bacchus. I'm sure of it. No one else wears clothes like that. He hated Sebastian. I'm sure it's his way of getting revenge."

"But Sebastian Merle is dead," Devon said. "What good is revenge now?"

Shelley threw up her hands. "Who knows?" she wailed. "Who knows how a crazy person thinks? But he was here, I'm sure of it." She gasped, pressing her hand to her mouth. "Wait, you don't think—did Bacchus kill Sebastian?"

Devon and Brianna glanced at each other. It gratified Brianna to see that Devon didn't indicate that he thought Shelley's idea was ridiculous. She vowed to herself to follow up with this new lead as soon as she could. Lennox shook his head.

"Let's not jump to conclusions, ma'am," he said placatingly. "I promise you, we'll explore every avenue. Now, better go make yourself a cup of tea, or something stronger, and we'll sort this out."

Shelley nodded and fled upstairs. Once the distraught woman was out of earshot, Brianna leaned toward Devon.

"Will you take Bacchus in for questioning?" she whispered.

"You know I can't share information about an investigation." Devon grimaced. "You'd better push off. We've got work to do."

Brianna waved goodbye and walked up the stairs. As she left, she heard Devon speaking to a detective on the phone.

"You're going to want to look at this. There's a likely connection to your case."

Brianna slowly rode home, thinking hard about the events of the day. In her mind, Bacchus had jumped from a potential person of interest to prime suspect. She needed to talk to him, and soon.

She whizzed down the last stretch of road into Snuggler's Cove. A few cars trundled along, looking for parking, and the light of restaurants spilled onto the road and through the dusky twilight. With a start, Brianna remembered she had a date with Troy that evening. She would have to hurry to arrive on time. This investigation—and her wine and cheese event—

were taking up a lot of her time, but she didn't want to push her burgeoning relationship with Troy to the side for them. Besides, she wanted to share the good news of a new suspect. Hopefully, this sabotage would take the heat off him.

Back at the marina parking lot, she quickly locked up her bike and strode to her bright blue float home with cheery orange trim. On the way, she dialed Macy's number.

"Did you find Bacchus's address?" she asked once they'd said hello and she'd given Macy a brief rundown of today's events. "I need to follow up with him, hopefully tomorrow at the latest."

"Got it," she said proudly. "He's down on Galleon Drive. I'll text you the number. Hey, tomorrow's my day off. Can I tag along?"

"Of course." At her door, Brianna fumbled in her purse for her keys. "Pick me up from the café at noon. But I've got to go now. I'm running late for my date with Troy."

"Ooo. Have fun."

Brianna hung up and dashed inside. She gave Paprika two minutes of cuddling until the cat had had enough and sauntered away. Then, she dashed to her closet.

Minutes later, she entered Gabriel's Pizzeria, panting a little. She patted her curls into place and glanced around the restaurant, looking for Troy. She found him at a window table, a candle in front of him and wine already poured. He looked peaky, and Brianna's heart went out to him. Being suspected of murder—on top of the upcoming competition—was a lot to handle. She hoped her news about Bacchus would make him feel better.

His face lit up when she approached.

"I hope you don't mind that I ordered some wine for you already," he said. "Since you seemed to really like the Chardonnay the other night, I got you a glass. I can order something else if you prefer."

"No, that's lovely." He was so thoughtful, remembering her preference. She settled into her seat and took a sip. "Delicious. Now, I have some good news for you."

Troy tilted his head. "Better than having you on a date with me?" he teased.

"I'll let you be the judge of that. I was at Orca Vineyards this afternoon, ordering wine for my event, and they discovered someone had demolished their cellar. Wine and glass everywhere."

Troy's jaw dropped. "Why would I think that was good news?" he whispered. "What a horrible waste. I didn't like Sebastian, but I adored his wines. He made really great stuff."

"No, you're right, it's terrible. That's not the good news. It's what they found at the scene." Brianna took another sip of her wine, relishing the telling. Troy's eyes never left her face. "They found a scrap of fabric snagged on the edge of a sharp rack. It had clearly been torn off the culprit's clothes. Shelley, the apprentice vintner there, she was convinced it was some crazy guy named Bacchus. Said he and Sebastian had a history, and it wouldn't surprise her if he were crazy enough to smash the bottles, and maybe even kill Sebastian.” Brianna raised her eyebrows. “So, the police have another, likely suspect in their case.”

Troy released his breath in a whoosh and covered his eyes with one hand. “Do the detectives know?”

“Yes, I heard the Mounties call the info in, and they told Shelley and me to leave them be while they investigated.”

Troy dropped his hand to the table and gave her a wobbly smile. “That’s great news. Oh, I hope they clear this up soon. I’ve been told to stay on the island until they tell me otherwise since I’m still a suspect and my name isn’t cleared yet.” He sighed. “Honestly, I’m not sure what to do. My sister’s wedding is next week, but I can’t attend if I’m not allowed off the island. If they finally have fresh evidence that points to the real killer, that’s amazing news.”

“I think that’s deserving of a toast.” Brianna held up her wine, and they clinked their glasses together.

The server came up and took their order. Troy let Brianna choose their pizza to share, and his consideration moved her. Once the server retreated, Brianna swirled her wine and spoke again.

“Have you ever heard of this Bacchus guy? He sounds like a wild one, but I can’t get a read on him.”

Troy snorted. “I’ve never met him, but a friend of mine went to one of his parties a few years ago. Bacchus invited him when he was walking his dog on the beach. There usually isn’t a rhyme or reason to the invites, as far as I know. My friend doesn’t remember much—too much wine—but he thinks he had a good time." Troy spread his napkin on his lap to prepare for their meal. "Bacchus ordered a barrel of one of my wines for his party this year, but only his partner was there when I dropped it off, so I didn't meet him. She's pretty intense. She has these eyes, you know." Troy widened his own, then he raised his hands to move around his head. "And the hair."

"Intriguing." Brianna chuckled and spread her own napkin as their pizzas arrived. The scent of melted mozzarella and fragrant tomato sauce almost drove thoughts of strange murder suspects out of her mind. Almost, but not quite.

She wanted to speak with Troy about her investigation but kept quiet. It was obviously upsetting to him—and rightfully so—and they were having such an enjoyable time. Devon's worried face flashed through her mind. No, telling Troy that she was planning to visit a potential murderer wasn't a good idea. She didn't want him to be concerned about her like Devon was. If she found out anything interesting, she would tell him then.

The café's phone rang mid-morning the next day. Brianna continued to pipe mascarpone icing onto moist beet muffins since Teri wasn't run off her feet. These purple-hued cupcakes wouldn't make themselves, and she'd promised a customer a box of two dozen for a birthday party to be picked up by three o'clock.

"Brianna? Phone's for you." Teri held out the café's

phone. Brianna sighed and wiped her hands on a tea towel, then took the receiver.

"Hello?"

"Brianna, hi. It's Devon Moore." Devon's deep voice flowed into Brianna's ear, and she straightened her spine. "I hope I didn't interrupt."

"Just baking. How can I help you?"

"I have that smoked fish to drop off, but I didn't think you'd appreciate it in the café's fridge." He chuckled. "It's pretty pungent. Can I drop it off at closing time one of these evenings, or at your house?"

"Closing would work." Brianna would have to distract Oaklyn when he stopped by, or she'd get another earful of kingfisher comments from the cheeky girl. "Thanks so much. Hey, what happened with the sabotage? Did you arrest anyone for it?"

"Not yet," he said. "The investigation is still ongoing. And you know that's all I can say."

"I understand." One side of her mouth twitched up. "I'll see you later."

Chapter 12

Macy picked Brianna up at two o'clock as promised, and the two of them tore down the road in her little red hatchback. Brianna cracked the window open to let the warm breeze trickle inside. The weather forecast threatened gloomy skies soon, but today, the sun shone for them.

"What's our goal here?" Macy said as she turned down Plank Way, the road that led to Galleon Drive. "I know we want to ask him questions and see if he's capable of destruction—or murder—but what are we pretending to do here?"

"His partner sells sculptures," Brianna replied. "We're looking at her art, maybe to buy."

Macy snorted. "You are, maybe. I don't have the money or the space in my house for sculptures. But sure, I can pretend."

"It's the only excuse I could come up with on short notice," Brianna admitted. "It will have to do. Look, there's the number."

Macy slowed down at Brianna's pointing finger. Each lot was big enough to hold a house, some towering trees, and a small field. The closest neighbor had a tall hedge bordering his property with a large vegetable garden sprawled beside a trim house. Bacchus's property was a different story.

"Driftwood sculptures?" Macy peered out the

windshield. "You're on your own for this one."

Brianna exhaled sharply as she gazed at Bacchus's property. The house with peeling brown paint looked like a stiff breeze could push it over, and the metal roof was so heavy with moss that the rust was barely visible.

In the front yard, bundles of driftwood taller than Brianna stood clustered into vague shapes. One might have been a heron or a drooping tree, and Brianna was almost convinced that another was an owl with outspread wings. Maybe. Shells and streamers of dried kelp decorated each one. Their size was impressive, but Brianna couldn't imagine many people having the space for one, or the interest.

The grass was dry and scraggly, and two donkeys sauntered in the backyard, with drooping chicken wire the only barrier to prevent them from escaping. After seeing Zola's antics, Brianna was certain they must have escaped regularly. A wandering footpath of loose stone slabs led past apple trees hung with wind chimes and suncatchers to a sagging front porch. Brianna looked at Macy, who shrugged.

"Time to go shopping?" Macy said.

Brianna wrinkled her nose at her friend and then exited the car. Grass brushed her calves on the way to the house, and the porch creaked ominously when she stepped on it. With a sharp rap, Brianna knocked on the door and waited with Macy beside her.

Shuffling footsteps sounded from an open window, then the door opened with a grinding noise. A portly man stood before them with a grin spread across his wide, round face. Graying stubble carpeted his double chin, and faint wisps of hair floated like a halo over his balding head. His eyes wandered over their faces with sleepy curiosity. A bare arm held open the door, and an off-white linen toga mostly covered the rest of his body.

Macy coughed to hide her inadvertent laugh. Brianna spoke quickly as a distraction.

"Hello. I was admiring your sculptures. Are they for sale? Not for me, unfortunately—no space at my house—but my in-laws would adore them. I thought I'd take a few pictures for them, if you didn't mind, then they can stop by here the next time they visit the island." Brianna stuck out her hand impulsively. "I'm Brianna and this is Macy."

"Oh!" The man looked taken aback. He shook her hand limply at first, then with increasing vigor. "Of course, of course. I'm Bacchus. Maenad's the sculptor, they're her work. Maenad!" he bellowed into the dark house behind him. "Customers!"

"Your in-laws?" Macy whispered to her.

"I couldn't stand Greg's parents," Brianna whispered back. "Imagining one of these sculptures in their tidy little yard gives me great pleasure. And they'd never visit here, so that loose end is cleaned up."

"She'll be here soon," Bacchus said to them with a dreamy smile. "We're busy preparing for the Bacchanalia tonight. We've been working like fiends all day. Haven't stopped."

Was that Bacchus's alibi for the sabotage? Brianna frowned. She'd have to confirm it with this Maenad person. Bacchus could have easily slipped away for twenty minutes while they were busy.

"That sounds like fun." Macy gave him a winning smile. "Your Bacchanalia, I mean. It's all about wine, isn't it? Will you be serving local wines at your party?"

Bacchus's face clouded over. "Some," he said sadly. "I was hoping for a barrel from Orca Vineyards. But that's all right. I don't mind. I bought a barrel from Whimsical Wines instead, and that will be splendid. Who needs Orca, am I right?"

"I'm sure it will be delicious," Macy assured him. "Did you have problems buying the Orca barrel?"

It was odd to see Bacchus's expression turn angry, like watching a normally happy toddler cry. It was a fleeting emotion, but transformative.

"Sebastian Merle told me I could have a barrel," he said, mashing his fist into his palm. "He told me—he said, 'You can have a barrel when Maenad sells a sculpture.' Well, she did, just last week, to a tourist from Squamish. Then what do you think Sebastian did?"

"What?" Brianna said.

"Took back his words! Laughed in my face! Told me he was joking, and there was no way he would ever 'sully his brand' by allowing me to serve his wine at my Bacchanalia." Bacchus heaved for breath, his face splotchy with red. "A verbal agreement, I call that. A promise. And broken with a laugh." He took a deep breath, and his face fell back into its smile lines. "Someone else in my situation might be furious, but I choose to let slights like that go. Especially when there are so many fine wines in the world. Whimsical will hit the spot nicely."

Macy glanced at Brianna with a pointed expression. Brianna agreed. Although Bacchus might have an alibi, his blow-up over the wine incident was suspicious. He clearly cared more about the Orca wine order than he pretended. If he was that angry when he was sober, what might he do if he was drunk? Kill a man?

Footsteps padded down the hall, and Bacchus turned to greet the newcomer. "Maenad," he said, his previous angst erased by his natural cheer. "Come show off your sculptures. These two lovely ladies are interested."

A petite woman wearing a shift of black linen stood beside Bacchus. Her black hair streaked with white was unbrushed with twigs and leaves stuck in it as if she'd been rolling around outside. Her eyes roved over Brianna and Macy as if sizing them up, then fixed on Brianna with an intense stare.

"You want a sculpture?" she said, her words clipped short. "Which one?"

"We're just looking," Brianna said with haste. "My in-laws might like them. I was hoping to take a few pictures."

Maenad waved toward the sculptures irritably. "Yes, yes, yes, fine. Go."

Brianna nodded her thanks, and she and Macy walked swiftly down the steps. Maenad disappeared back into the house, but Bacchus tottered out after them.

"You should come to our Bacchanalia," he said to them. "Tonight. Oh, please, say you'll come."

Macy stopped dead and whirled around. "Us? You

want to invite us?"

"Of course!" Bacchus threw up his hands. "Bring your beaus. The festivities start at eight and end at dawn. Come ready to party!"

He laughed, a deep rolling laugh that came from his belly, and wandered around the back toward the donkeys. Brianna stared after him, but Macy grabbed her arm.

"Let's do it," she said with excitement. "Oaklyn's at a sleepover tonight, and I don't have work tomorrow. It's been ages since I went to a party, and his are legendary."

"I don't know," Brianna said. Late-night booze-fests really weren't her thing. She wavered at the look on Macy's face. Macy had given up a lot when Oaklyn had come along, such as the chance to do carefree things like all-night parties.

"We could keep investigating," Macy wheedled. "Maenad looks like a suspicious character."

"You think so?" Brianna had wondered about the surly woman. Bacchus might have provided the motivation for her to act.

"Meh, not really. I just want you to say yes."

Brianna grinned. This was a chance to see the two suspects under the influence, which might be illuminating. "Fine, we'll go. What does one wear to a Bacchanalia?"

What with the investigation on top of her usual

baking and business duties, Brianna's wine and cheese event planning had fallen off the rails. To remedy this, she spent the rest of the afternoon riding around, sourcing decorations and extra napkins. Her event shouldn't suffer just because someone had had the terrible plan of murdering Sebastian Merle. She could do it all—investigate, run her business, plan an event, and go to a party—she just had to knuckle down.

When her phone pinged from her bike basket, Brianna pulled over to the side of the road and checked the message.

Just thinking about you, Troy had written.

Brianna's stomach fluttered.

Me too, she wrote back. *See you soon?*

Once this competition is over, I'm all yours.

Brianna tucked her phone away, still smiling, then continued on her way. She rode past the laundromat with her basket full of supplies. A car door slammed across the road, and Brianna turned to see who it was. She shook her head at herself—she would be as bad as gossip-loving Hilda Button after a few years on this island—but she looked, anyway.

Drusilla Silverleaf stalked across the road with a black garbage bag slung across one bony shoulder. She thrust out her jaw and marched into the laundromat. A bell tinkled when the door opened.

It must have been laundry day for Juicy. Brianna continued to ride, then pulled over to the sidewalk with a frown. Why would Juicy bring her clothes to a laundromat? She owned her own house, and surely she had her own washing machine inside. Did her clothes need mending, or perhaps, have a stubborn stain that wouldn't come out without professional help?

Brianna wouldn't have cared except that Juicy was one of her prime suspects. Anything the other woman did out of the ordinary interested Brianna.

She dropped her kickstand and meandered toward the laundromat. When Juicy strode out of the shop a moment later, Brianna feigned intense interest in pet supplies in the next store's window. Juicy didn't even glance her way. She drove off a minute later, and Brianna wandered inside the laundromat.

A row of washing machines and dryers lined one wall, but the shop offered a myriad of other services, too, like carpet cleaner rentals, mending services, and photocopying. At the counter, two women were discussing the bag that Juicy had left them. A rounded, middle-aged woman with close-cropped gray hair pulled out a garment from the bag that a younger woman with pink hair held out for her. Brianna stepped closer on the pretext of examining a carpet cleaning machine.

"What was she doing in this shirt?" the older woman muttered. "I think it was white, once, but you wouldn't know it to look at it now."

"What is it?" the younger woman asked. "It's sort of purple. Did she spill some ink?"

"I don't know. She wouldn't say." The older woman sighed and shoved the shirt back in the bag. "Maybe ink, maybe grape juice. It's going to be a nightmare trying to get it out, that's all I know. It probably can't be done, but we'll have to try it." She noticed Brianna for the first time. "Sorry, I didn't see you there. Can I help you with something?"

"Just looking for a price list," Brianna invented. "For your laundry services."

The pink-haired woman handed her a printed sheet with a list of their offered services. Brianna thanked her and walked quickly out of the shop, her heart hammering. Juicy's clothes were covered in juice stains. Had she been sloppy while making her fruit wines, or was this evidence of her involvement with the sabotage at Orca Vineyards?

Chapter 13

Brianna adjusted her top—a sparkly number she'd kept for years, although she'd rarely had the opportunity to wear it—and spoke into her phone.

"I know it's odd, but I promised Macy I'd go. You're sure you don't want to come with us?"

"I wish I could, but I'm swamped here tonight." Troy sounded genuinely regretful. "But you should go have fun with your friend. And I want to hear all about this notorious party later." He chuckled. "As much as you can remember, that is. Call me if you need a ride."

Brianna's heart warmed at Troy's offer, his encouragement, and his trust. Greg had always been more interested in doing what he wanted than giving any thought to Brianna's desires. She was glad she'd started dating Troy. Maybe there were more fish in the sea for her, after all.

She thanked him and they hung up. Brianna smoothed down her shirt one more time, then grabbed a sweater to combat the cool night air and padded down her stairs. She and Macy were bicycling to the Bacchanalia since they didn't want to worry about drinking too much. Bicycling under the influence wasn't technically allowed, of course, but Brianna figured she'd cause a lot less damage slowly trundling home on her bike than getting behind a wheel. The island was a quiet place after dark.

Brianna pulled over to the side of the road by Macy's house, one half of a rundown duplex in the same neighborhood as Quentin. The grass was shaggy, and the windows needed cleaning, but Macy had a cheery pot of chrysanthemums beside the door to liven the threshold.

Macy came traipsing out a moment later. Brianna chuckled. Her friend must have been watching from the window to be outside so quickly.

"Wow," Brianna said. "I feel underdressed."

Macy had wriggled into a tight minidress of a vibrant fuchsia that hugged her slender body well. Long silver earrings dangled from her earlobes, and her makeup had transformed her from a preschool teacher to a nightclub star.

"Come on. I never get to dress up. I'm taking this opportunity with open arms."

"Don't let me stop you." Brianna glanced at her own sparkly shirt, which now felt decidedly demure. "Maybe I should have found something more daring."

Macy giggled and carefully clambered onto a rusty pink bike a size too small for her. She adjusted her dress with a grimace.

"It's Oaklyn's old one," she explained when she caught Brianna eyeing her ride. "She wouldn't dream of touching anything pink these days, of course. I haven't ridden a bicycle for years, but I'm sure it's just like riding a bike."

Brianna laughed and pushed off the curb, Macy behind her. They rolled down the road, and Macy teetered for a minute but soon got her bearings. They pedaled gently down a few quiet back roads, going slowly so they wouldn't arrive with their party clothes all sweaty. Bacchus's house wasn't too far from Macy's.

It was clear where the party was. Loud music erupted from the property and was audible from the main street. An orange glow lit the night sky, and an occasional donkey heehaw drifted through the air. Laughter and hooting beckoned them up the driveway. The Bacchanalia was in full swing.

Brianna stopped her bike and stared with misgiving at the commotion in Bacchus's backyard. Macy laughed.

"You should see your face. Come on. You'll feel better after some wine. And we can leave anytime. You know I've got your back."

Brianna took a deep breath and exhaled a chuckle. "It's been a while since I partied. Okay, I'm ready. Let's do this."

They tucked their bikes along the fence and wandered with unsure steps into the backyard. The sky was clear and filled with pinpricks of light, a fortunate break for the cool autumn evening.

A donkey stared mournfully at her as she passed its enclosure, although it had a small pile of carrots, apples, and other donkey treats to munch on. Past the donkeys, frequent tiki torches illuminated a vista of tables and people, and a bonfire raged in the center of the lawn. Thumping bass vibrated through Brianna's chest from a speaker against the ramshackle house.

"My new friends!" Bacchus stumbled toward them with a metal wine goblet in one hand. He beamed and held out his arms like Brianna and Macy were his long-lost daughters. "You came! Welcome to our Bacchanalia."

"Thanks for inviting us," Brianna said. She cast about for something to say. "You were lucky with the weather."

"Rain, shine, it doesn't matter. One year we wallowed in the mud like pigs. The gods bring the rain and the sun." He waved toward the revelers, and wine sloshed out of his goblet. "Eat, drink, and be merry. Tonight is a time for celebration!"

"What are we celebrating?" Macy asked with a smile.

"Life!" he roared.

He tottered away. Brianna and Macy glanced at each other. Then they both burst out laughing with their hands over their mouths.

"I need some of whatever he's having," Macy gasped. "Where's the wine?"

"Over there." Brianna pulled Macy's elbow, as eager as she was to indulge a little. She knew the wine would be excellent since Troy had made it. "I was hoping to get some evidence that Bacchus did—you know what—but I really can't see it. At least, not when he's drunk."

Macy snorted. "No way. Not enough coordination, for a start. Keep your eyes on Maenad, though. She might have done it for Bacchus. I hear she's devoted to him, although you wouldn't think it to look at them. She organizes this whole shindig because he wants it, and she plays along with his god delusions. I don't know what their story is."

"Good point." Brianna grabbed a glass of wine. A

toga-wearing older man who looked like an ancient Roman senator was filling glasses from a barrel with the Whimsical Wines logo. She cast her eyes around the party, where many others had embraced the dress theme. "Where is Maenad, anyway?"

Macy joined Brianna in looking at the crowd, then coughed into her glass. "Is that Hilda Button?"

Brianna followed her gaze and her breath caught. It was definitely Hilda—for once not darning a sock—along with Magnus Pickleton. Behind them, Esme Alonso had donned a form-fitting toga-like dress with a tiara of golden grape leaves on her head and was draped over a handsome man with a square jaw and salt-and-pepper hair. They laughed with Obi and Quentin Flagstaff, the latter the most relaxed Brianna had ever seen him. His bowtie dangled out of his trouser pocket, and he drank his wine with energetic mouthfuls.

"The whole cheese club is here," Brianna said in wonderment.

"I thought this thing was more exclusive," Macy said. "I feel slighted that this is the first year I was invited." She giggled. "Just kidding. Happy to be here. Come on. Let's wander around."

They circled the bonfire. Maenad had certainly pulled out all the stops with the décor. A large cement fountain featuring naked cherubs had been set up on the edge of the lawn, a spread of finger food took up three trestle tables, and enough torches dotted the grass to rival the stars above. Macy picked up an olive as they passed the food.

"Sticking with the theme," she said with a smack of

her lips. "How very Mediterranean."

"Brianna!" Hilda hailed her then hiccupped. She put a dainty hand against her mouth. "Oh my, this wine is excellent. I didn't know you'd be here. How lovely. Isn't this a wonderful party?"

"Party, my foot." Magnus eyed Hilda balefully, then took another drink of his wine. "What's it even for, I ask you. All these fires everywhere, someone's bound to light themselves up. And the wine!" he roared out suddenly. "Why is it gone again?"

He tipped his cup upside down and shook it. Only a few drops fell out. He stumped away to find more, his steps slightly uneven.

Hilda tittered, her own stance not as surefooted as usual. Brianna led her to a chair, and she sank into it.

"You two look like you're having fun," Brianna said with an amused glance at Macy. "Do you have a ride home?"

"My daughter's coming to pick me up," Hilda said with a wave. "She'll take that old lush, Magnus, too. Just you wait, he'll deny he was tipsy tomorrow. Ha! What a bag of hot air."

Hilda smiled indulgently and hummed to herself, seeming to forget Brianna was there. Brianna straightened and joined Macy in looking over the celebrations. A small puppet stage nearby featured roughly made puppets acting out a questionable story as onlookers roared with laughter. On the other side of the bonfire, an acrobat wearing a bright blue stretchy bodysuit stood on his head and juggled beanbags with his feet.

Macy grabbed two more cups from a passing tray and handed one to Brianna. Brianna was surprised that her first glass was already empty. Troy did make excellent wines.

"Cheers," Macy said. "To good times and good friends."

They clinked glasses. Brianna sipped her wine, feeling pleasantly buzzed and at peace with the world. She knew she should look out for suspicious behavior from Maenad—or anyone else—but it was hard to muster up the interest. She deserved a night off, didn't she? The case would still be there tomorrow. Troy's stressed face swam through her mind. She shook the image away with a guilty toss of her head. Tomorrow, first thing. Tonight was for fun.

"Look." Macy squinted across the bonfire. "Isn't that Corporal Devon Moore?"

Brianna's head whipped around so fast that her wine-soaked head wobbled. She blinked hard and focused on the line of Macy's gaze. Sure enough, Devon's dark head, strange without his Mountie cap, bobbed across the fire.

"Ugh, Cecelia Yang is with him." Macy blew a raspberry. "I never imagined Cecelia turning up to a thing like this. I thought she was way too sophisticated for that." Macy drew out the word "sophisticated" with an obnoxious drawl.

Brianna chuckled then squinted again. "There's Maenad, finally. Talking to Cecelia."

The two women were speaking. Maenad gestured around the lawn, and Cecelia looked sulky. She put a hand on her hip and pointed at herself and Devon. Devon edged behind her, as though trying to disassociate himself from the conversation.

With the two women standing next to each other, their relation was obvious. Maenad's hair, although streaked with gray and not nearly as sleek as Cecelia's, was the same texture and color. They shared the same tiny frame and petite features, and even their scowls were identical.

"Is Maenad related to Cecelia?" Brianna asked.

"She's Cecelia's mother," Hilda piped up from behind them. "My understanding is that Maenad gets Cecelia to come to the Bacchanalia through skillful guilt-tripping. She likes her daughter to show support. No one ever accused Maenad of having a soft touch, unless Bacchus is involved." Hilda tittered. "There's an odd couple, if I've ever seen one."

"Would Maenad do anything for Bacchus?" Brianna asked carefully. Just because her head was fuzzy didn't mean she couldn't exploit an opportunity for information when she found one. Macy glanced at her but kept quiet.

"Oh, I expect so." Hilda settled herself more comfortably in her lawn chair. "She drove all the way to Edmonton to buy those donkeys, you know, because he wanted them. Rescue animals, I think. But he'd do anything for her, too." Hilda sighed dramatically with her hand on her chest. "True love. My George was just the same, bless his soul."

Devon's gaze scanned the crowd and landed on Brianna. His eyes lit up, and his shoulders visibly relaxed. When Cecelia's mother dragged her into the house, both women gesticulating furiously, Devon wandered in Brianna's direction.

"I didn't realize you'd be here," he said when he reached them.

"We received an invitation from Bacchus himself." Macy lifted her glass. "How could we refuse a summons from the god of wine?"

Brianna laughed. "I'm gathering that invitations aren't as exclusive as some people make them out to be."

"Is that a dig?" Devon's eyes twinkled. "Aren't I a worthy supplicant to an ancient god, reincarnated on earth?" He glanced over at Bacchus, who sat on a bench with two others, roaring with laughter and sloshing his wine all over the grass.

Brianna laughed. "I don't know how much wine he's getting in his mouth anymore, and how much is spilling on the ground."

"Well, no one said revelry was dignified."

A hissing noise crackled from behind them, then a sound like gunfire exploded. Devon grabbed Brianna by the shoulders and whirled her around so he was between her and the noise. She froze, pressed into his side, feeling the heat from his body against her back.

"Fireworks!" Macy clapped her hands. "Oh, how beautiful."

Devon released his breath. Only then did he seem to realize he was clutching Brianna to him.

"Sorry about that," he muttered. "Too much emergency training. The instincts take over."

"Better over-prepared than under," Brianna responded. She straightened her sparkly shirt, unsure of what to say. Devon had put himself in harm's way for her, and she didn't know what to think about that. To move past the awkward moment, she asked, "I saw Cecelia and Maenad together. That's her mother, right? They didn't look happy."

"A tense relationship, from what she's told me." Devon glanced at the house. "I don't know whether Cecelia wants to hug her mother or throttle her, most of the time. I don't think she knows. She didn't want to come tonight, but her mother insisted. But, Cecelia was here helping Maenad and Bacchus prepare the decorations all morning about a week ago. I can't keep up."

"Relationships can be tricky," Brianna agreed. Her brain processed what Devon had said. "A week ago? That's a lot of preparation for this party. What day was that?"

"Monday, I think. Cecelia had the day off. She was here with the two of them all morning until lunch." He scrunched up his face in thought, then his eyes narrowed and he looked at her in suspicion. "Why do you ask?"

"Just wondering." Brianna tried to look innocent.

"You're still investigating," he accused her. "Were you thinking that Maenad and Bacchus had something to do with Sebastian Merle's death?"

"I was just curious," she said with an attempt at innocence. When he continued to stare at her, she sighed. "After Shelley saw the linen scrap at Orca

Vineyards, I wondered if the two events might be related. I honestly don't think Bacchus has it in him to murder someone, but Maenad needed a closer eye."

Devon sighed and rubbed his face. "You're not letting this go, are you?"

"Nope."

"Fine. Yes, the detectives have already examined these two, for the exact same reasons you concluded. Their alibi on the day of the murder checks out, though. They're still under suspicion for the sabotage, but there's not enough evidence to hold them yet." He crossed his arms and glared at her. "Happy?"

"Not until we find the killer." Brianna stared out at the crowd. "But I'm happy that Bacchus didn't do it. He's growing on me."

They watched the rotund man heave himself to his feet and roar happily for Maenad. She materialized from the house, while Cecelia stood in the doorway watching, and strode over to Bacchus. He grabbed her and whirled around in time to the beat of the music. After a fraction of a second, Maenad relaxed. The ghost of a smile crossed her face, and she joined Bacchus in a wild, ungainly dance around the bonfire.

Brianna laughed and exchanged an amused glance with Devon. More people joined in the dance, and even Macy grabbed a man's hand and pulled him into the circle. He looked surprised but gratified by her attention, and Brianna grinned when she caught her friend's eye.

"Are you going to leave a woman waiting?" Hilda chirped at Devon. She was on her feet, her cane forgotten beside her chair. "I might be old, but I still have a dance or two left in me, young man."

"May I have this dance?" Devon said formally, a smile tugging at the corner of his mouth.

Hilda took his hand, then grabbed his waist and yanked him toward the bonfire. Devon gave Brianna a helpless look then whisked the elderly lady into the swirl of people. Hilda hooted, and Brianna laughed hard. The stars twinkled overhead, past the burning fires, and Brianna couldn't imagine a more unlikely, or a more welcoming, place to be.

Chapter 14

Brianna eventually got roped into the dance circle by a cackling Macy. They alternately whirled around and drank wine from the never-ending trays that materialized between songs. By the time they stumbled away from the party in the deep of night, Brianna's head was swimming and the world was fuzzy.

"Don't tell Devon we're riding home," she whispered loudly to Macy. "We're drunk-pedaling."

Macy collapsed into giggles. "If I hit a raccoon, I'm blaming you." She hiccupped. "You're a bad influence."

"Me?" Brianna tried for a tone of outrage, but she couldn't keep it up before laughter took over. "Come on, you drunkard. I don't think I can balance. We'll have to push the bikes."

Giggling and weaving, they walked down the deserted road into town. The stars looked brilliant now that the Bacchanalia's fires had subsided into a dim glow behind them. The pounding music faded, and Brianna filled her lungs with the air of a chilly autumn night. Over the crest of a hill, the sea lay black and vast leading out from Snuggler's Cove. Suddenly, Brianna longed for her cozy bed and the purring warmth of Paprika, who had taken to keeping her company while she slept. She had a lot to think about tomorrow, but her brain wasn't up for it tonight.

Brianna woke to the beat of furry paws kneading her cheek. When she opened her eyes, a fuzzy orange face stared at her and meowed.

"Ugh," Brianna grunted. Someone had stuffed her head full of wool while she was asleep. "Is it breakfast time for you already?"

Her bleary eyes landed on her bedside clock. Three minutes until her alarm was due to ring.

"I suppose I should thank you for being considerate," Brianna murmured as she scratched the cat's chin, "but it's hard when my head is foggy. We'd better get a move on. Cats and bread wait for no woman, no matter how little sleep she got the night before."

Brianna fed her hungry little beast, dressed, drank extra water and a large coffee, and was out the door a few minutes later. She had extra time this morning, thanks to all the preparation she'd done the day before. Bread dough waited in the fridge, rising slowly all night long, and dry scone ingredients were pre-mixed and ready for liquid to be added. Maybe she should do this every day. This was the time normal people rose and greeted the day.

She shook her head then regretted the motion. No, most days she preferred to wake before everyone else. Something about the quiet calm when only birds chirped soothed her.

But she was glad for her preparation today. She locked the door of her float home and strode down the dock.

A familiar figure stood at the end of the wharf, and Brianna raised a hand in greeting.

"Hi, Corinne," she called to her fellow float home dweller. "Off to work?"

"And dropping the kiddo off at school." She motioned to her tow-headed son, who was having an animated discussion with a fisherman preparing his motorboat for the day. "Mason loves talking to everyone we meet. We leave early so I don't have to rush him."

"That's sweet." Brianna yawned. "Sorry, I was up late last night. Sometimes it's hard being a baker."

"I don't think I could manage it." Corinne waved when Mason waggled his hand at her. "Mason gets me up early enough. Baker's hours have never sounded appealing."

"It's certainly not for everyone."

Now that Brianna was fully awake, she glanced at Corinne with a critical eye. Corinne was still a suspect in Sebastian's murder, in her books. Someone had set up Bacchus to take the fall. Could it have been Corinne, trying to take the heat off herself? Time for a little sleuthing.

"Did you hear about the sabotage at Orca Vineyards?" Brianna asked in the casual, gossipy tone she'd been honing during her investigation. It had proved useful time and again. "Someone went in there and smashed a bunch of wine bottles in the cellar. It was a terrific mess."

"I heard about that," Corinne whispered. "Tuesday

morning, wasn't it? It's disgusting. How vindictive. What was the point? Random vandalism? Or someone with a vendetta? It doesn't make any sense, especially now that Sebastian Merle is dead. It's only going to hurt whoever's taking over the winery." She shook her head in sorrow.

Brianna suppressed a sigh. Either Corinne was a superb actor, or she had nothing to do with the sabotage. And she'd made excellent points to boot.

"I wish I'd been there to see who'd done it," Corinne said. "I deliver packages to Orca a few times a week. But it was reading day at Mason's kindergarten, and I couldn't resist volunteering."

That alibi would be easy to confirm. Brianna's tongue played with her teeth while she thought.

"Yes, terrible," she echoed. "What a waste."

"Alicia," Corinne called out. "Good morning."

Brianna turned to see the red-headed realtor looking stylish in a fitted blazer and pressed trousers, her teenage son Joel at her side. She waved at the approaching pair, and Joel nodded at her.

"We don't often see you out at this time, Brianna," Alicia said warmly. "You're usually the early bird."

"I went to the Bacchanalia last night," Brianna admitted sheepishly. "It was a late one."

Alicia laughed heartily. "Oh, I'll bet. I'm surprised you got any sleep at all."

"Even old people like you can party?" Joel said to Brianna with a grin. His mother smacked his arm, but Brianna laughed.

"Occasionally. We regret it the next day, though."

"Oh, Corinne, I meant to ask." Alicia checked her phone. "Yes, it's Thursday. If that package arrives for me today, do you want to join me for coffee again when you drop it off? We had such a lovely visit last Monday during your delivery."

"Maybe a short one," Corinne said. "We spent most of the morning gabbing last time. I barely got my deliveries in before picking up Mason from his after-school care. But sure, that sounds nice. I should be there by ten o'clock, just like last week."

Monday of last week? Brianna nodded to herself with equal parts satisfaction and disappointment. Corinne had been with Alicia the morning of Sebastian's murder, so it couldn't have been her. Unfortunately, that meant Brianna was no closer to finding the real murderer. She needed to gather her information—and her wits—to track down this elusive killer.

She said goodbye to everyone and walked to the Golden Moon. Teri hadn't arrived yet. Brianna washed her hands and aproned up quickly. She stirred together two large batches of scones to start the day, then she took the cheese bread dough and croissants out of the fridge for proofing. With any luck, the scones would be done by the time the café opened, and Teri would have something to serve hungry customers.

A sliver of leftover Camembert beckoned from the fridge, and Brianna munched it during the brief respite between baking bouts. She hadn't eaten breakfast yet— too busy and too hungover—but now that she'd been up and about, with water and coffee in her system, everything looked much rosier.

Teri arrived and flipped the front door sign to Open to start their day. One of the first customers through the door was Macy. She'd pulled her shoulder-length hair into a rough ponytail, and dark shadows circled her eyes.

"You look awful," Brianna exclaimed. "Park yourself somewhere. I'll get a coffee straightaway."

"How can you be so horrible and wonderful at the same time?" Macy dropped into a wooden chair near the counter exit. "My head is about to explode from the combination. Or maybe that's my hangover."

Brianna ran to pull her scones out of the oven and deliver them to the front counter for Teri. Then, she turned on the espresso machine and prepared Macy's coffee with a dash of vanilla the way she liked it.

"Over here," Macy moaned. She grabbed the drink from Brianna then stared at her with baleful eyes. "How are you so perky? You drank the same as me!"

"I've been up for an hour already, and my second coffee is already down the hatch."

"Braggart," Macy muttered. "I saw Devon Moore riding his horse this morning like he wasn't at the party last night either. Must be his day off. Why on earth doesn't he spend it sleeping instead of cantering around like headaches aren't a thing?"

Brianna's stomach gave a little twist at the image of Devon riding his retired Mountie horse, Sarge. It must have resulted from watching a Jane Austen film the other night and seeing gentlemen ride elegantly across the English countryside. She waved at the counter.

"Scone?"

Macy turned a paler shade of white and shook her head. "Give me a minute."

Brianna tapped her fingers on the table, mentally counting. She'd been thinking while she baked and as the caffeine worked its way through her system. She needed to solve this mystery to get Troy off the hook; otherwise, he'd be stuck on the island indefinitely when his family needed him at his sister's wedding.

"I talked to Corinne Bletchley this morning," she said quietly. "You know, the delivery woman with a grudge. Turns out she has an alibi for the murder, so she's out."

"We're doing this, are we?" Macy took another fortifying sip of her coffee then straightened up. "Okay. I'm ready."

"And we learned last night that it's not Maenad and Bacchus, either." Brianna drummed her fingers on the table. "Who does that leave us with?"

"My bet is still Quentin Flagstaff," Macy said at once. "Just follow the money. You said he looked shifty. Plus, remember, he was trying for a loan at the bank. It just makes sense." She sniffed. "If you're the murdery type, that is."

"He's definitely a prime suspect," Brianna agreed. "But don't forget Drusilla Silverleaf, from Duchess Row. The bone she had to pick with Sebastian was the size of a T. rex femur, and she has a temper to boot."

"Oh!" Macy sat up straight. "I forgot to tell you. I talked to one of the parents at my preschool yesterday, and she said that her sister is a neighbor of Duchess

Row."

"And—"

"I'm getting there." Macy glared at her, but her yawn and subsequent chuckle softened the expression. "Ugh, today will be tough. Anyway, the sister said that there was glass on the winery's driveway, and she swore she saw the label of a bottle from Orca Vineyards lying in the gravel."

"What does that mean?" Brianna said slowly.

"Either Drusilla was having her own party the other night, or she was still in a rage over Orca." Macy raised a knowing eyebrow at Brianna. "You know, after the sabotage. Why else would she have had a bottle from Orca on her property? With the bad blood between them, I can't imagine she would pay for a bottle at the store, and Sebastian surely wouldn't have given her one."

"Stranger and stranger," Brianna said. "Drusilla is definitely entrenching herself on my suspect list."

"And you said Esme Alonso was acting oddly."

"I don't think she's the culprit—" Brianna started.

"But could she have information?"

Brianna stared at her friend in consideration. "She might," Brianna admitted. "Okay, so Esme is due for a visit. If she can help guide my way at all, I need her. Time is ticking for Troy. Even if they haven't arrested him yet, he needs this settled. His sister is getting married next week, and he can't attend if he's stuck here, waiting for the investigation to wrap up."

"I noticed Esme likes your poppy seed gruyere crackers," Macy said with a smack of her lips. Her cheeks now held a hint of color. "Treats are your best currency for information."

Chapter 15

Once Macy had left and Brianna had finished her café baking, she hastily threw some crackers into the oven. When the timer went off, she whisked them out and dropped them in a baking tin with the lid off so they would cool. Then she hopped on her bicycle and tore down the road toward Esme's house.

It hadn't taken Macy—the fount of all knowledge— long to find Esme's home address. Her house wasn't far from the village, and Brianna had hardly broken a sweat by the time she turned onto Arbutus Road. A familiar figure stood on the corner, and she stopped to say hello.

"Brianna, dear." Hilda Button waved cheerily at her from a white lawn chair at the car stop. Driftwood Island had no bus service, so instead of bus stops, the island had frequent car stops where anyone driving by could offer a ride to waiting pedestrians. Hilda took advantage of the service frequently. Brianna suspected it was less from the need for transportation, and more from a desire for fresh gossip.

"Hello, Hilda. Sorry I can't offer you a ride, but this is a bicycle built for one."

Hilda chuckled. "My bicycling days are long over. A car will come along soon, no doubt. And until then, I have my sock to keep me busy." She held up her latest project, a large green sock with yellow dragons stitched across the front. "The wait will give me time to finish this."

Brianna wondered, not for the first time, who the recipient of all these socks was. She imagined the grimace of some middle-aged son of Hilda's receiving a care package from his elderly mother with another pair of exuberant socks inside.

She had more important issues on her mind than Hilda's sock obsession, though. Quentin's alibi needed verifying, and who better to ask about the comings and goings of the Bumblebee Bed and Breakfast than the owner herself? Hilda didn't concern herself with the details of running the place, but nobody passed Hilda's observant eyes unnoticed.

"Hilda, I know it's a long shot, but do you remember Quentin Flagstaff coming in for breakfast at the Bumblebee last Monday? Were you in that day?"

"Monday?" Hilda rested her sock in her lap and stared at Brianna thoughtfully. "Yes, I believe so. I was resting in my chair in the restaurant dining room. My joints had been acting up, so I was taking the morning easy. Rosy took my granddaughter to preschool that day. But no, I would have noticed Quentin."

A car crunched on the road's gravel shoulder. Hilda turned and waved at the driver who got out of the car to help Hilda into the passenger's seat.

"There's my ride," she said. Brianna helped her out of her chair, and Hilda shuffled toward the car. "Have a lovely rest of your day, dear."

Brianna waved Hilda off as she filed Quentin under "prime suspect" in her mind. Then she continued down the road toward Esme's house.

A minute later, she dropped her bike on the lawn of an all-white, Art Deco style house with a flat roof. Windows along its smooth front allowed a view of the ocean through sparse trees across the road. Brianna walked up the paver walkway lined with boxwood hedging and rang the doorbell. A Persian cat watched her from the shadows of a wooden Adirondack chair on the porch while she waited.

The door flung open at Brianna's second knock. Esme stood on the threshold, wearing a flowing dressing gown in a vibrant, geometric-patterned silk. She'd tied it loosely at the waist, exposing a fair amount of skin. Esme, true to form, held herself with unabashed poise. Brianna felt a twinge of jealousy at the older woman's self-confidence.

"Esme, hi." Brianna came right out with it. "I need your help."

"Of course you do, darling." Esme stepped back and ushered her in with a languid wave. "What with?"

Brianna followed Esme down a dark hall lined with oversized abstract paintings, plush carpet in a vibrant teal hue, and chocolate brown wainscoting. They passed a dining room with rounded cushioned chairs and a dangling chandelier of twisted metal spheres, ending up in a bright sunroom at the back of the house, where creeping vines and fan-like fronds of tropical greenery lined the edges. In the center of the room was a bistro table with two wrought-iron chairs. Brianna perched on one while Esme grabbed a mug from the nearby kitchen cupboard. She settled in across from Brianna, who offered the tin of baked goods.

"Oh good." Esme plucked a cracker from the tin and popped it in her mouth. "It pays to know a baker. Now, let me pour you some tea—I just made it, so it's fresh—and tell me how I can help."

Brianna sipped the tea Esme offered her in a black bone china mug with a gold rim. The floral liquid had a surprising taste, and she looked into her cup with interest. Her eyes widened at its rich blue color.

Esme laughed. "Never had butterfly pea flower tea before? It's from South Asia. You can really taste the lemongrass they add, too." She picked up her own mug and sipped. "Now, what is it you wanted to talk about?"

"It's Sebastian Merle's murder," Brianna said. She set the mug on the table. "There are some loose ends that need tying up, and only someone in the know about the winery dynamics on the island can help—someone without a stake in it."

Esme's eye twitched, but her face was otherwise impassive. Brianna wondered what the reaction meant.

"You've come to the right place." Esme stretched her legs out comfortably, letting her gown slip a little further up her thigh. "Ask away."

"I don't understand what happened with Drusilla Silverleaf and the award competition. Troy Winchester said that Drusilla entered before Sebastian died, but she swears up and down that she doesn't care about awards, and that Sebastian never would have let her enter anyway because of his grudge against non-grape wines. What's the real story?"

Esme stared at her for a long moment. Brianna

maintained eye contact. What was going through Esme's mind? Brianna hadn't thought the question a loaded one.

"Promise not to tell anyone," she said at last.

"Tell anyone what?" Brianna shook her head in confusion. "If it's something to do with the murder, I might have to tell the police."

Esme waved her hand airily. "I don't care about them. The Mounties are mostly tight-lipped, and the detectives aren't from around here. No, you can't tell anyone like Hilda. Gossip would be all over the island like wildfire. You know how she babbles to everyone within earshot."

"I can definitely promise that." Brianna leaned forward.

Esme glanced around with a guilty expression, as if worried that eavesdroppers were lurking among her potted plants. In a stage whisper, she said, "I took a bribe."

Brianna blinked. A bribe wasn't murder, but it was shady. What had possessed Esme?

"In my defense," Esme continued, "it was for a good cause. Sebastian was lobbying the board to disallow alternate-fruit wines from the competition. He couldn't stand the thought of Duchess Row wines sitting on the same table as his own bottles." Esme leaned back and crossed her arms. "Old, misogynistic, closed-minded codger is what he was. Don't get me wrong. He has a point. Grape wines are in a league of their own, and while I enjoy Duchess Row's fruit wines, they're not truly in the same class. But I disliked

Sebastian's vendetta against Juicy. When she approached me, offering a sizable sum to vote against Sebastian's proposal in the upcoming board meeting," Esme shrugged, "I took it. Bought myself a lovely pair of designer stilettos with the cash."

Brianna sat back, processing this new information. "Bribery?" she said at last. "Unethical, but not murder. Still, if Juicy was willing to bribe her way into the competition, that tells us two things."

"That she's willing to bend her moral code," Esme said with a sip of her tea.

"And that she desperately wanted to enter the competition, which means she lied to me." Brianna drummed her fingers on her lap. "What else did she lie about?"

"Juicy was fired up at Sebastian," Esme said with a knowing glance. "Fit to be tied, really. I'd say she would do anything to get back at him after he started lobbying against her. She wouldn't take no for an answer, not when it came to entering the competition. Juicy has a vindictive streak."

"What makes you say that?"

Esme took a long sip of her tea while Brianna waited. She was clearly relishing the suspense.

"Last year," Esme said finally, "Juicy was dating somebody from the mainland. He would come over on the weekends. It didn't last long. Fair enough. I mean, I couldn't stand Juicy for long, either. Anyway, he broke up with her. They'd only been dating for a couple of months, but she went ballistic. The neighbors heard the screaming from down the street. He drove to the ferry—couldn't wait to get away, I imagine—and went to the café next door until the ferry boarded." Esme leaned forward. "Bruce—he works for the ferries—he told me that when the man came back, someone had scratched his car to smithereens. The sides had been keyed, terribly so. A beautiful old Aston Martin, apparently. And the security cameras weren't working—as usual—so they never found the culprit." Esme leaned back and took another sip of her blue tea. "But I think we can all guess who did it."

Brianna digested this story. "So, it wouldn't be out of character for someone like Juicy to smash all the bottles at Orca Vineyards in a fit of vengeful rage."

Esme raised her eyebrows. "Is that what happened? No, that wouldn't be out of character for Juicy. Not at all."

Brianna ran a finger back and forth along her mug's handle. If the fruit-wine vintner had keyed her ex-boyfriend's vintage car, it wasn't so far-fetched to imagine her swinging a sharp corkscrew at Sebastian in a fit of rage. She wasn't the strongest-looking woman, but adrenaline was a powerful force, and Sebastian wasn't a large man. She could have dragged the body into the vat with enough motivation. Brianna swallowed.

"Thanks for the tea." Brianna stood. "And the food for thought."

"Remember your promise." Esme looked at her sternly as she rose with Brianna. "Not a word to anyone, except the police if you must. I have no intention of playing favorites when judging the wines. I only wanted to allow Juicy to enter the competition if she wanted to. Call it female solidarity, if you will. She deserved a fighting chance, instead of being steamrollered by that odious vintner. Truth will out, for wine quality, but it was only fair that we gave her a chance. And my new shoes really are stunning."

Brianna said her goodbyes. When she mounted her bike and pedaled into the road, she pursed her lips in thought. Drusilla Silverleaf was becoming a prime suspect, although too much of Brianna's evidence was hearsay and character profiling. She needed hard evidence to bring to Devon and the detectives.

And Quentin Flagstaff wasn't yet out of the running, especially with what Macy had overheard at the bank and Hilda's assurances that his alibi was false. Brianna pedaled harder toward the bakery. She needed to restock her baking tin. Once she had her ammunition, she would have time to be neighborly and stop by Quentin's for a visit.

Chapter 16

The café was busy that afternoon, and Brianna pursed her lips. Not that she minded the extra customers, but what had brought them all here?

She smacked her hand against her mouth. Of course. How could she have forgotten? It was cheese wheel day.

In August, she'd started a monthly tradition. A delivery of one large wheel of cheese would come rolling into her café, and she would use the opportunity to educate her customers about the particular cheese variety, as well as create a minor spectacle to draw people in. Hopefully, they would purchase a few scones and coffees while they were there.

Brianna checked her phone. Sure enough, the delivery truck was almost due. She wheeled into the alley, locked up her bike with haphazard motions, and burst into the side door of her kitchen.

Oaklyn was dabbing at her heavily made-up eyes. They were red-rimmed and moist.

"What's wrong?" Brianna asked, concerned. Oaklyn liked to portray an unflappable exterior, but Brianna knew from experience that the teen years were fraught with tears.

"I'm fine." Oaklyn gave her a brittle smile. "Something got caught in my eye."

The girl clomped into the dining room to take care

of a customer. Brianna stared after her, worry lacing her thoughts. Then she sighed and pushed Oaklyn's concerns away. She couldn't force the girl to open up to her. Well, she could try—for Macy's sake, if for nothing else—but it would have to wait until after the cheese wheel had arrived.

Brianna quickly changed into her cheese café tee shirt in the bathroom and then entered the dining room after Oaklyn. The café tables were almost full. Groups of parents with young children loudly chattered along one side, and a few tea-sipping elderly friends gabbed in the corner. She checked the time again. Only a few minutes until the wheel arrived. Should she make an announcement now or wait until the truck was here?

While she dithered, Oaklyn sidled closer to her.

"I saw Rob," she said, her voice thick. "With Hannah. They were walking into the movie theater last night. Holding hands."

Driftwood Island's only movie theater was the main hangout spot for the town's teens on Wednesday nights when popcorn was free. Brianna's heart squeezed tight at the pain in Oaklyn's voice. She'd been so excited about dating Rob—Brianna could tell even through the girl's carefully crafted bored façade—and now her hopes had been dashed in such a cruel way, being lied to by the person she was opening her heart to. Brianna felt crushed on Oaklyn's behalf. Honesty was paramount in a relationship.

Brianna only wished that Oaklyn had seen the signs of Rob's betrayal before it had shown itself so blatantly. To someone with more experience, the red flags had been waving: poor excuses, not showing up when promised, no clear expectations about their status. But only experience would teach Oaklyn that, and Brianna only hoped that this lesson would make her wiser, not harden her.

"I'm so sorry, sweetie," she said, wrapping an arm around the girl's shoulder. "Nothing hurts like a lie."

Oaklyn turned her face into Brianna's shoulder to hide her tears from the room. Brianna rubbed her back for a minute. Then, when Oaklyn's body stopped shuddering with silent sobs, she patted her arm.

"Go on," she said gently. "Clean yourself up. I'll take over the counter for now."

Oaklyn nodded and averted her face with its ruined makeup while she hurried into the kitchen. Brianna sighed heavily then hitched a smile on her face for an approaching customer.

"Good afternoon, and welcome to the Golden Moon. What can I get for you today?"

While Brianna poured hot water into a teapot and dished out a slice of cheesecake onto a fresh plate, a white delivery van pulled into the loading space out front. Brianna quickly finished with her customer then walked out from behind the counter.

"Excuse me, everyone." She spoke loudly to the room. The chatter died down, and people turned in their seats to look at her. "Today is a special day. It's the day when the Golden Moon receives its delivery of a new product. I'm pleased you are here to witness the rolling of a giant Camembert, because it's Cheese Wheel Day!"

The crowd cheered. Brianna grinned and strode to the front door. A patron held it open for her, and she walked out to greet the delivery person. Corinne Bletchley smiled at her.

"Special delivery for Brianna West." She held out a clipboard. "Sign here, and I'll grab it."

Corinne disappeared into the back of her van and staggered out with an enormous disk the size of a child's bicycle tire wrapped in white paper. Brianna handed back the clipboard and carefully lowered the cheese wheel to the sidewalk. Then, with slow, stately steps, she rolled the wheel into the café.

Customers craned their necks to look at the wheel. Some pointed it out to their neighbors and exclaimed over its size. A young girl stared at the wheel. Brianna grinned at her. When she got to the front, Oaklyn was behind the counter again, her makeup freshly applied and a determined smile on her face. Brianna winked at her then heaved the wheel onto the counter.

"Thank you all for joining us today to witness the new Camembert wheel delivery," she said to the room. "This magnificent cheese originally hails from France but is now enjoyed all over the world. With its solid rind and creamy center, you can enjoy it baked in the oven and spread over garlic bread, sliced and melted into panini, or simply spread on a cracker. In a few minutes, we'll pass around samples of the wheel so you can taste it for yourselves."

Brianna hefted the wheel in her arms and placed it on a large cutting board set up for this event. She unwrapped it with ceremonial slowness, and the delectable smell of ripened Camembert wafted past her nose. Customers peered at the wheel as she worked. Brianna couldn't keep a smile off her face. She busied herself cutting small slices of the cheese and arranging them on two large platters for sampling, then she picked one up and sailed toward the tables.

Oaklyn took the other platter, and they spent the next five minutes passing out samples. Brianna educated her customers further on different ways to cook and eat Camembert, and she was pleased to hear Oaklyn doing the same. Her employee had been paying attention for the past few months, it seemed. The distraction was good for her. The girl's face was more animated than usual, and she even smiled indulgently at two little boys who thanked her for their cheese samples.

A teen boy about Oaklyn's age sat in the corner with what looked like his younger sister and mother. The three waited patiently for their samples, but Brianna noticed that the boy's eyes never left Oaklyn. Brianna hid her smile and left the table for Oaklyn to cover. The girl would have to work through her heartbreak, but on the other side, there was plenty to look forward to.

Once Brianna had handed out all the Camembert samples, the cheese wheel crowd dispersed and left a more typical number of customers in the café. Oaklyn was calmer now, too—the cheese wheel event had soothed her earlier despair—and Brianna felt confident in leaving the café under the teenager's command, with Annalise next door as backup.

She pulled a few Asiago scones out of the counter display and placed them alongside the chunk of Camembert in her baking tin. Once she'd pushed her trusty red bicycle onto the road, she pedaled hard toward Quentin's house.

When she arrived in front of Quentin's small bungalow in the neighborhood east of Snuggler's Cove, she paused to let her heart slow its pounding beat. This probably wasn't a smart idea, interviewing a murder suspect by herself. She could hear Macy's shouts in her mind, her friend's voice mingling with Devon's deeper tones, both filled with worry for her.

But she needed to know about Quentin. Troy was depending on her, with his sister's wedding only days away and the case lingering on without resolution. Quickly, she dashed off a text to Macy saying to expect a call from her in half an hour, and to send backup to the Flagstaff household if Brianna didn't call.

That job done, Brianna took a deep breath, grabbed her tin of baking, and marched to the front door. When nobody answered it, she cautiously followed the side path into the back garden.

"Hello? Anyone there?"

Quentin poked his head around the corner. Between his round glasses and wide-eyed surprise, he looked like a startled owl.

"Brianna?" He pushed his glasses further up the bridge of his nose. "Hi. What brings you around?"

"Just passing by, thought I'd say hello, be

neighborly, you know." Brianna held out the open tin to Quentin. "It was Cheese Wheel Day at the café, and we received a wheel of Camembert. It's quite nice. I thought you might like to try it."

Quentin still looked confused about why Brianna was here, but he dutifully plucked a slice of cheese out of her tin.

"Mmm," he said after a moment's reflection and chewing. "That is nice. Really creamy and intensely flavored."

"I thought so, too."

"Too bad Obi isn't here. He loves Camembert. But he's away for the night on a wellness retreat on Cedar Island. Meditation and all that."

Brianna pursed her lips. How could she gently bring the conversation around to the murder? She didn't have Macy's tact. All she had were her facts, her suppositions, her sense of when others lied, and her baking. They would have to do.

"Actually, Quentin." She shuffled her feet then planted them firmly on the ground and looked him in the eye. "I do have something to ask you. I'm still looking into the murder of Sebastian Merle. My friend Troy Winchester is a prime suspect, for lack of better evidence, but I don't believe he did it. I'm looking for evidence to support his innocence." She cleared her throat. "Some things you've told me are untrue, so now I don't know what to think. Why did you lie about needing money? My friend saw you inquiring about a loan at the bank. And your alibi for the murder doesn't check out. I asked Hilda Button, and she doesn't remember seeing you at the Bumblebee. Where were you that Monday morning?"

Quentin's forehead beaded with sweat, and he looked everywhere except at Brianna. She half expected him to bolt.

Then he sighed heavily and ran a hand across his forehead. His shoulders drooped, and he looked at Brianna with miserable eyes.

"Yeah, we need the money," he said, "but Obi doesn't know it yet. I'm a graphic designer, and I lost my biggest client. It was my fault, too. I forgot to deliver their logo design—I thought I'd sent it and hadn't—so they fired me. They were going to be a big part of my income for the next few months, and now they're gone. I haven't had the heart to tell Obi."

"Thank you for your honesty." Brianna stood her ground, although her heart pounded. Was this a confession from Quentin? Was he telling her he'd killed his uncle for the money?

"No, no." Quentin waved his hands wildly. "You misunderstand. I didn't kill Sebastian. I'm not that desperate, and I'm not a murderer. He was a bastard to most, but he was always good to me. As for the alibi," he swallowed, and his Adam's apple bobbed, "I wasn't at the Bumblebee like I said. I was at Madame Tremblay's." He dropped his eyes with a shame-faced air.

Brianna stared at him. "Should that name mean something to me?"

"She's a psychic," he mumbled to the floor. "I went to get my tarot cards read. Obi thinks it's all hogwash, and I'd never hear the end of it if I told him." He looked up defiantly. "But I had to do something. I need to find new clients, and I thought she could help guide me."

Brianna sighed. "Can we call Madame Tremblay to confirm that?"

Quentin took Brianna's offered phone and typed in a number with shaking fingers. As it rang on speakerphone, they both stared at the device.

"'Allo. Madame Tremblay, truth-seer," said a deep, purring voice.

"Hello," Quentin said. "This is Bob Brown. Can you remind me the date and time of our last appointment?"

"Bob Brown?" Brianna mouthed at him.

"I used a fake name so it wouldn't get back to Obi," Quentin whispered.

"You visited on Monday morning, the seventeenth of September," purred Madame Tremblay. "Now, may I book you another appointment?"

"Not today, thanks." Quentin said.

Brianna hung up and shoved her phone back in her pocket. Not only had her internal lie detector not flared up during Quentin's confessions, but his alibi checked out. Brianna could safely cross him off her suspect list. "Thanks for being honest, Quentin. And I'm glad you didn't kill Sebastian. I didn't enjoy suspecting you."

Quentin leaned against the stucco of his house, looking drained. "It's terrible being suspected of murder. The police are still watching me, but they don't have enough to bring me in."

"You should tell them what you told me. An alibi is

key to taking yourself off their list." Brianna checked the time on her phone, her heart sinking. "Unfortunately for Troy, time to find the real killer is running out. He needs to get off the island for his sister's wedding in a few days, and the police won't let him leave yet because he's still under suspicion."

"If you want to solve the mystery, go to Drusilla Silverleaf." Quentin stood upright and snapped his fingers. "Wait. I saw her the morning of the sabotage at Orca Vineyards. I was driving by Bacchus's house—it's on the way to a friend's place—and I saw Drusilla getting in her car and driving away. What was she doing there? She had no reason for being there. They aren't friends, and he didn't serve Duchess Row wines at the Bacchanalia."

"They found a strip of Bacchus's toga at the destroyed cellar," Brianna murmured. "It felt like a setup, especially after I met Bacchus. Drusilla's actions would explain the fabric. She could have stolen a piece of a spare toga to plant at the scene when she smashed the bottles."

"And she has motives coming out of her ears," Quentin added. "So much hate bottled up in one person."

"She has no good alibi," Brianna added. "And I saw her dropping off wine-stained laundry at the laundromat the day after the sabotage at Orca Vineyards. Coincidence?"

They stared at each other. Brianna's mind whirled with facts and guesses. This was it. She finally felt confident that she had enough information to present to Devon Moore. She needed to head to the Mountie detachment immediately.

"Thanks for your help," she said to Quentin. He took another piece of Camembert before she put the lid on her baking tin. She turned back when she reached the corner of the house. "I recommend you tell Obi everything. Lies in a relationship are poisonous."

Quentin hung his head. "I will," he agreed. "But if you see me sleeping at the community hall for the next week, you'll know why."

Chapter 17

Brianna pumped her pedals up the hill to the Mountie detachment, fueled by her determination to tell Devon everything she'd learned. This was it. Drusilla Silverleaf was almost certainly the murderer. And with the vindictive vintner behind bars, Troy could leave the island as he pleased, unencumbered by the doubt of the police and town.

Brianna shoved her bicycle in the municipal hall's bike rack and raced inside the Mountie detachment. Lennox, sitting at the front desk, looked unsurprised to see her.

"You're here to see Corporal Moore, right?" He turned around at her nod and shouted down the hall, "Devon, someone here for you."

Brianna twisted her fingers in a nervous twitch until Devon appeared in the hallway. His eyebrows rose when he spotted her.

"Brianna," he said. "What can I help you with?"

"I have information about Sebastian Merle's murder," she blurted out. "I need to speak to you."

Devon's mouth thinned, and he gave her a look of exasperated amusement. "Really?" he murmured when he drew closer. "I thought you were going to put that aside."

"Nope, I never said that." She danced impatiently. "Are you interested in what I have to say or not?"

"Always." He ushered her into the hallway. "But let's tell the detectives at the same time."

Brianna stopped and blinked at Devon. "Can't I just tell you?" she stammered. "I don't want to bother the detectives. I'm sure they're busy."

What she really meant was that she didn't want to encounter a Greg-lookalike. Her late husband had been a detective in Vancouver, and his viewpoint had always been that Brianna had no place in his business. What if these detectives were cut from the same cloth? Her information was too important to be brushed aside.

"They'll make time for a valuable source," Devon assured her. "I'll be there, too. Come on, they're right through here."

Brianna dragged her feet behind Devon as he strode to a closed door halfway down the hallway. She dreaded speaking to the detectives. She feared they would share Greg's face and demeanor, give her a patronizing smile, and ask for a coffee while they discussed their important work.

Brianna squared her shoulders. She could do this. Even if they were clones of her late husband, she had important information. She would make them listen.

Devon opened the door and motioned for her to enter the room before him. She took a deep breath and walked inside.

A tired-looking man with a wrinkled shirt over his paunch sat at a conference table, looking at a tablet with a grimace on his worn face. Across from him, a woman with sandy blond hair in a ponytail tapped her pen against a stack of papers with a frown of concentration.

Both looked up with relieved expressions when Brianna and Devon entered the room. Were they happy to be distracted from their work? Brianna took their demeanors as a good sign. Hopefully, they would hear her out.

"Detective Branson, O'Sullivan," Devon greeted the man, then the woman. "If you have a minute, I'd like you to meet Brianna West, a local business owner. She has information pertinent to the Sebastian Merle case."

"Good," Branson muttered. "We could use a break."

"Nice to meet you, Ms. West." O'Sullivan pulled out a chair from beside her. "Please, sit down. As my colleague mentioned, any extra information you could tell us would be helpful."

Brianna sat next to the female detective with far more composure than she thought she'd have in this room. So far, they hadn't treated her as a child. Would they take her conversations seriously? There was only one way to find out.

"Thank you, detectives." She kept her back straight. Devon nodded at her as he leaned against the wall by the door. "I've taken a keen interest in Sebastian Merle's murder, and through speaking casually with my friends and neighbors, I've gathered some circumstantial information that might fill out your notes."

"Ms. West has successfully helped us in the past," Devon added.

O'Sullivan raised an eyebrow. "We are certainly open to any information you can give us."

Brianna laid out everything she had found so far, no

matter how small the detail. Quentin's visit to the psychic, Esme's bribe-taking, the stories of Juicy's past and of her laundromat visit, Corinne Bletchley's alibi… she left nothing out. Hopefully, her information, when combined with whatever evidence the detectives had scrounged up, would be enough to put the real culprit behind bars.

The two detectives gave each other significant looks. Brianna twisted her hands in her lap under the table.

"Thank you for your time," O'Sullivan said to Brianna. "We appreciate you coming forward with this. We will do our due diligence and take all the evidence into account."

Brianna could recognize a dismissal when she heard one, so she stood and followed Devon out the conference room door. Once it closed behind them, she heaved a sigh of relief.

"You never cease to amaze me," Devon said as they walked down the hall and into the front entrance of the detachment. "You found out all that information on your own? The detectives have been working for days and they haven't narrowed it down like you have."

"I have my ear on the ground." Brianna grinned at him. "And I'm friends with Hilda Button, the incurable gossip. It's amazing what you can find out if you just listen."

Devon glanced around once they were outside. "It's not my place to say," he murmured, "but with the information you gave today, this investigation might be wrapped up soon."

Brianna's heart swelled. Had she brought justice for

Sebastian Merle's death, and exonerated Troy at the same time? She could get used to this feeling of pride in her chest.

Brianna rode home in the dusky twilight feeling like someone had filled her with helium. Even if it didn't happen today, Drusilla Silverleaf would soon pay for her crimes—murder, sabotage, framing an innocent man—and Troy would be free and clear. Once again, justice would be served.

She decided to treat herself for dinner and stopped at the pizzeria. Fifteen minutes later, she balanced a pizza box in her basket and wheeled slowly through Snuggler's Cove to the marina. Tonight, she would celebrate with Paprika. Tomorrow, she would visit the wine competition briefly to show her support for Troy, and then she would focus all her energy on setting up her wine and cheese event for that evening. Despite the murder investigation slowing her preparations considerably, she was almost ready for the Friday evening event. She hoped it would be the talk of the town, but for that to happen, she needed to knuckle down tomorrow and get her act together.

Paprika meowed when Brianna opened the door. She rubbed herself against Brianna's legs.

"Hello, princess." Brianna bent down to stroke Paprika's head. "I missed you, too."

Paprika sniffed at the pizza box then gave it an experimental swipe with her paw.

"You're welcome to try a piece of chicken from my pizza," Brianna said with a chuckle, "but I think you'll like your dinner better. Come on, let's get our food."

Paprika meowed her agreement, and they moved into the kitchen of Brianna's little float home. Paprika jumped onto a kitchen chair and watched Brianna with her ginger tail twitching, while Brianna found her can opener and prepared the cat food. Once Paprika was taking dainty bites from her food dish, Brianna flopped onto the couch with her pizza box and a cold glass of Riesling from the bottle she'd opened the day before.

Her phone caught her eye. Troy should know what had happened at the Mountie detachment. Nothing was certain, but knowing that the detectives were homing in on Drusilla would take a weight off his mind.

She picked up the phone and dialed his number, her heart beating a little faster than usual. She wanted to be the one to tell Troy the heat was off him.

The phone rang until Troy's voicemail kicked in. Brianna hung up without leaving a message. She would tell him the good news tomorrow at the competition. Hopefully, it would be a day full of good news for Troy.

Brianna woke to a mouthful of ginger fur. She turned her head away from the warm lump on her pillow and wiped off her tongue with her pajama sleeve.

"When I let you sleep in bed with me," Brianna muttered, "I wasn't expecting to share my pillow."

Paprika ignored her and continued to slumber

peacefully.

Brianna stretched her arms over her head. It was luxurious to sleep in, especially since it happened so rarely. Six days a week, her alarm woke her up—before dawn in the growing darkness of autumn—and she trundled her way to the café to bake. But today, on this very special Friday, she'd made it known that the café would be closed. Her wine and cheese event was tonight. She planned to support Troy at the competition in the morning and prepare for her evening event in the afternoon. Customers might be disappointed to miss their morning treats, but business was good these days, and she didn't want to be a slave to the café if important things were happening in her life.

Through the skylight window of her loft, Brianna watched a blaze of color sweep across the morning sky as if a giant paintbrush had washed the fleecy clouds with watercolors of brilliant orange, vibrant pink, and mellow purple. A jet crawled across the sky, and the streaming vapor of its passage shone a stark white against the bright background.

Brianna soaked in the beauty for a few minutes, her mind blissfully blank. Thoughts eventually crept in as she awoke fully. The events of yesterday traveled through her mind, and she examined each tidbit as it floated by.

Drusilla Silverleaf had killed Sebastian Merle. Brianna still wasn't sure how she had overpowered Sebastian, since she was such a slight woman. Maybe Sebastian had turned around for a moment? Although, that wasn't likely if they were arguing. Sebastian could have stumbled and given Drusilla time to grab the corkscrew, she supposed.

And then, there was the issue of getting the piece of Bacchus's toga cloth. Quentin Flagstaff had seen Drusilla leaving Bacchus's road, but how had she snuck into his house? As far as Brianna knew, the winery owner and the god-wannabe had no social connection.

The fruit vintner had a motive, though. Brianna threw back her blankets and stood, stretching again. Drusilla's rage at Sebastian could have fueled a murder, and certainly the destruction of Orca's cellar. Had the detectives found any other evidence that would put Drusilla away for good? They had been tight-lipped about the investigation in her presence, as Brianna had expected, but the looks they'd exchanged were promising. They'd clearly felt that the information Brianna had brought them had value.

Brianna dressed and wandered downstairs. She cracked two eggs leisurely into a frying pan and put toast into the toaster. Normally, she ate a scone at work when they came out of the oven, but her day off was worthy of eggs on toast. She debated warming up some pre-cooked sausages from her tiny freezer, but when the toast popped up, she changed her mind. Her food was ready, and she was hungry.

She bundled into a blanket and braved the cool morning air on her little deck. The smell of salt and the lapping of wavelets against her home soothed her as she nestled into her deck chair. The sun was up properly now, and its beams warmed her beautifully.

She couldn't relax fully, though. Something was bothering her. Was it simply her desire to tell Troy about recent developments? Maybe. She could also ask his opinion on Drusilla. Troy hadn't wanted to talk much about the murder investigation, but now that Brianna was sure the detectives had a clear culprit, maybe he could relax and discuss it with her.

Brianna stuck a fork into her eggs with gusto. Yes, chatting with Troy about this would ease her discomfort. Keeping clear lines of communication between two people was the basis of a good relationship, in her opinion. She was cautiously optimistic about Troy's place in her life in the future and wanted to grow that relationship further.

Chapter 18

When Brianna arrived at the community hall later that morning, the grounds had a festival air to them. Vendors had set up tents for an autumn outdoor market, with stalls selling everything from carved wooden bowls and pottery to freshly baked loaves of bread and heaping baskets of fruit. People wandered among the tents, eating caramel apples and laughing at the juggler entertaining them. A musician with a guitar warbled folk music on a makeshift stage on the side.

At the community hall, however, events were far more serious. Somber volunteers in black trousers and burgundy tee shirts wore nametags and greeted interested visitors at the open door. A printed sign hung on the wall announcing the nineteenth annual British Columbia Wine Awards.

Brianna shook her head. The market looked like fun, but she wondered at the decision made by the town council to hold the two events at the same time. She understood wanting to make the competition a big deal, but they clashed rather magnificently.

Nevertheless, she promised herself that she would find the cinnamon bun seller once she'd greeted Troy. A few people had walked by with them, and her stomach told her in no uncertain terms that her eggs and toast were long gone.

She walked up the steps and received a pamphlet

from a grave volunteer with graying hair and blue-rimmed glasses.

"The judging starts in half an hour," the woman said in a gravelly voice. Her glasses winked in the sunlight. "The award ceremony will begin once final decisions have been made. You may greet the vintners while judging is in process."

Brianna thanked her and wandered inside. The small entrance hall where visitors usually left their coats was bare except for a magnificent display of pumpkins, fall flowers, a large wicker cornucopia, and other festive decorations. The double doors leading to the main hall were open wide. Covered tables lined one wall, and rows of folding chairs gathered around a small stage made of risers and a draped cloth with a podium on top.

The tables held bottles of wine, and Brianna recognized some labels. Whimsical Wines had a good number present, as did Duchess Row. Many other wineries were represented, but Brianna didn't see any from Orca Vineyards.

Brianna looked around the milling crowd, spotting Esme across the room. The woman waved her fingers at Brianna but continued to speak with her companion, a suave older man dressed in a suit with a bright red handkerchief poking out in a perfect triangle from his vest pocket. Troy was at a table filling out some paperwork and hadn't seen her yet. Brianna scanned the crowd but saw no sign of Drusilla Silverleaf's lank brown hair and oversized glasses.

"I thought the wines each needed a representative,"

a passing volunteer mentioned to his friend. "Someone dropped off Duchess Row last night, but the owner isn't claiming them today."

"I heard she's in a spot of trouble with the police," the woman accompanying the volunteer murmured with a significant look at her companion. "We'll see if she turns up."

Had Devon and the detectives arrested Drusilla Silverleaf already? Was she currently in custody? Brianna couldn't help a smile crossing her face.

A familiar figure wandered nearby, gazing at the bottles on display. Brianna walked over to him.

"It's Mike, right?" she said. "From Orca Vineyards?"

"Brianna." He greeted her with a smile under his mop of brown hair. "You must really be a wine connoisseur to attend a stuffy event like this. It's incredibly important for the wineries involved, but it's not a spectator sport."

"A friend of mine entered," she said. "I'm here for moral support."

"Me too."

"I didn't see any Orca bottles on the table." Brianna scanned the rows again in case she'd missed them.

Mike shook his head. "No, I decided not to enter them. Too much flux at the winery right now, what with the boss being gone and all. The paperwork would have been a nightmare because he can't sign it. And for what? The new owners, whoever they will be, can handle the awards when they take over. It's not my worry now." He jerked his head at the bottles. "It will give the other entrants a fighting chance for an award, anyway. I don't want to brag, but Orca always swept the table at this sort of event. We do bottle a great product."

"It is delicious," Brianna agreed. She was happy to hear that Troy would have a good chance at winning an award this year.

A strange scent of burned grass wafted past her nose. It smelled so familiar. What was it?

She gave another experimental sniff, and Mike chuckled.

"Sorry about that." He sniffed his sleeve. "Yeah, that's me. Sebastian always insisted on burning sage in the fermentation room. Said it infused the juice with a savory flavor that couldn't be beat. His secret sauce, if you will. We were all sworn to secrecy, but it's not like he's going to go after us now." Mike sighed. "I still don't believe it myself, but I don't not believe it either, you know?"

"So you burned it anyway?" Brianna guessed.

"Yeah. The first of the grape harvest came in this week, and I couldn't break the habit of lighting the sage this morning. Can't hurt, right? I don't know if the health inspector knows about it, but it's only in the fermentation room, nowhere else." Mike waved at someone across the room. "I'd better go. It was nice chatting with you, Brianna."

Brianna said her goodbyes, but her mind was elsewhere. She'd smelled that unusual scent recently. When had it been?

She shook her head and walked toward the bottle table, where Troy was nervously twisting his wines so the labels were exactly facing out. His face was twitchy, and he kept fiddling with each wine bottle.

Brianna bit her lip. Troy seemed so nervous. This competition was such a big deal for him and his winery, and she fervently hoped he won at least one award.

He jumped when she touched his elbow, then gave a tremendous sigh of relief. "Brianna, it's you. You startled me."

"Evidently."

A blast from an air horn at the festivities outside rang out clearly. Brianna blinked at the noise, but Troy jumped and accidentally hit one of his bottles. He caught it as it angled toward the floor, and instant beads of sweat stood out on his forehead.

He carefully pushed the bottle back into place, his fingers trembling. Brianna placed her own hand on his when he adjusted the bottle again.

"Why don't you take a break with me in the back?" she said gently. "We can sit and take deep breaths. I have some good news for you, too."

Troy stared at the wines, then he nodded and gave her a forced smile. "That's probably wise."

Brianna took his hand in hers and led him to the back of the hall. One door led to a small side room, and Brianna poked her head in before they entered. Benches and more folding chairs lined the walls, but it was empty of people, so she pulled Troy inside and shut the door. Noise from the chattering crowd outside dulled to silence, and Troy took a deep breath.

"Sorry," he said sheepishly. "I guess I'm a little stressed."

"It's a big day for you," Brianna said soothingly. She perched on the edge of a bench and pulled Troy down with her. "I understand."

"You said you had good news?" Troy tilted his head at her. "What's up?"

"Oh, yes. You know Drusilla Silverleaf, the owner of Duchess Row?" When Troy nodded, Brianna squeezed his hand. "I won't bore you with the details, but I'm pretty sure she's not here today because they arrested her for Sebastian Merle's murder."

Troy's fingers tightened in hers, and his face grew pale.

"Seriously?" he stammered. He blinked a few times. "That's great news. They found enough evidence to detain her?"

"Yes." She smiled at him. "And that means you're out from under the microscope. How does it feel to be a free man?"

"Amazing," he murmured, staring across the room with a shocked expression. "I can't believe it."

Brianna gave him a moment to process the information. Her mind wandered back to the strange smell emanating from Mike this morning. Where had she smelled it before? Had the scent been on Shelley during her Orca Vineyards tour? But nothing had been burning during the tour. She'd smelled it days before.

Brianna's eyes widened. That was it. She'd smelled the burned sage scent in the café the day she and Dot had visited Orca Vineyards, just after she'd heard the news about Sebastian.

The smell had come from Troy.

Chapter 19

Her fingers squeezed involuntarily in Troy's, and she willed herself to relax them while her mind feverishly ran through her revelation.

Troy told her he had visited Orca Vineyards that morning, but he'd been insistent that he hadn't been inside the building. But according to Mike, Sebastian only ever burned sage in the fermentation room because of his desire for secrecy. Unless Troy had suddenly started burning his own sage at Whimsical Wines, he could only have immersed himself in that strange smell at Orca Vineyards' facility.

Why had he lied to her about going inside the building? Brianna ran through other notions. Troy had been quick to point fingers at Esme Alonso and Maenad. She hadn't been able to get a hold of him on the phone during the bottle destruction at Orca Vineyards. And his nerves lately had been disproportionate to the competition's importance, in her mind.

Brianna bit her lip so hard it almost bled. Bacchus had served Whimsical Wines at his Bacchanalia. Troy had told her he'd delivered the barrels early in the morning the day of the sabotage. He could have easily stolen a piece of Bacchus's toga fabric while he was there to frame the old wine enthusiast.

Brianna extricated her fingers from Troy's hand

slowly, to not startle him.

"Troy," she said slowly. Her eyes raked his face. "Please answer me honestly. Did you smash the bottles at Orca Vineyards, and plant a piece of Bacchus's clothing at the scene to frame him?"

If it were an unfounded accusation, Brianna was in danger of destroying her budding relationship with Troy, the healthiest one she'd had in years. But if it were true...

"What are you asking?" Troy said indignantly, but the beads of sweat returned, and his panicked eyes darted over her face. As he stood to face her, Brianna's heart shriveled into a ball of horror and betrayal. "You can't honestly believe I would do something like that."

"This competition means a lot to you." Brianna clenched her fingernails into her palms. "And there's potentially a lot of money on the line. Did you do it just so you could win a few awards?"

"It's more than just a few awards," he hissed and started to pace. "Winning this competition would rocket Whimsical Wines into the big leagues. Orca is already there. Sebastian didn't need any more accolades. He could share."

"It's not about sharing. It's about letting the best wines win." Brianna stared at Troy, watching the man she had been growing to care for sloughing away until a lying stranger paced in front of her. "How could you ever think that destroying Sebastian's wines was worth it? Did you—"

She stopped, horrified by what she'd almost accused him of out loud. The meaning hung in the air between them. Troy's face twisted.

"I didn't mean to kill him," he wailed suddenly. Anguish wracked his face, and he gripped his hair in both hands. "I went to see Sebastian to talk about the competition, to see what categories he was entering. He yelled at me and then disappeared into his barn. I followed him to give him a piece of my mind, and he led me to the fermentation room. We kept arguing, and he got so mad that he lunged at me with a racking cane. Those things are heavy—I had to defend myself. I grabbed the nearest weapon I could find—a corkscrew on a nearby barrel—and I swung it at him." Troy covered his eyes with his hands. "He wasn't young, and he couldn't avoid it. The tip stabbed right into his temple. He fell, and—" Troy swallowed.

"And that was that," Brianna finished for him. She was surprised at how steady her voice was. "But why did you put the body in the vat?"

"There was no evidence," he moaned. "I'd even been wearing my motorbike gloves, so there were no fingerprints. And so many others hated Sebastian. It was easy to cast suspicion on someone like that clown Bacchus. Then the tide turned and everyone suspected Drusilla Silverleaf. It wasn't hard to smash an Orca bottle on her driveway to frame her." He looked at her, pleading for her to understand. "The competition was so close. You don't understand. I need this. And with Sebastian out of the way, it just made sense to smash the bottles so Orca would be less likely to enter the competition."

Brianna could feel her heart breaking despite her

calm exterior. She'd thought she and Troy had been going places, but he was as much a lying jerk as Greg had been. Worse, even. For all his faults, her late husband had never killed someone.

How had she been so blind? Her self-confidence withered into nothing. How could she rely on her intuition when it could so clearly lead her astray?

"You can't let Drusilla take the fall for your mistake," she said firmly. "Let's go to the police right now. If you confess, the judge might be more lenient with you."

Troy stared at her, a vein twitching in his forehead.

"No," he whispered and moved toward her. "I wish you hadn't stuck your nose in this."

Panic blazed in his eyes. Brianna realized what he was about to do the second before he did it. She opened her mouth to scream for help, but his large hand clamped her mouth shut.

She bit down and felt flesh between her teeth. Troy cursed but didn't let go. Despite her frantic wriggling, he wrapped his other arm around her torso and held tight. The well-built frame and strong arms that she had so admired in the past now worked against her. She struggled, but Troy was implacable.

"I need to get through the competition first," he panted in her ear. He dragged her to the side of the room. "Then I'll figure out what to do with you. Awards first."

He wrapped a leg around hers to secure her while he fumbled with the handle of a cupboard door. Inside, tablecloths and other linens hung on poles and hooks.

A few extension cords lay on the floor. Troy bent them both down to pick one up. On the way back up, he grabbed a cloth napkin and shoved it in Brianna's mouth. She gagged as the rough fabric touched the back of her tongue.

Troy deftly wrapped the extension cord around her arms then another one at her ankles. He tied them up with knots that Brianna recognized, and she nearly cried at the perfect bowlines. In a different life, they could have gone sailing together on her aunt's dinghy. The future she'd been cautiously imagining for them—for herself—exploded into dust and blew away, leaving her shivering and alone.

"Now stay quiet until I fetch you later," Troy said, shutting the closet door. The only light came from a crack at the bottom of the doorframe.

Brianna slumped against the soft tablecloths, breathing heavily through her nose and trying not to panic. She couldn't stay trapped in this closet until Troy came back for her. Now that he'd lied so thoroughly to her, she couldn't trust anything he said. She would never have thought he could harm her, but she would also never have thought he could kill someone and cover it up, all to promote his business. Who knew what he would do with her after the competition ended? If he let her go, she would run straight to the police, and he knew that.

She had to escape. Easier said than done, of course. It would be easiest to shout for help, but the gag prevented that. She spent a fruitless minute trying to push the soggy fabric out with her tongue, then by scraping her face against a tablecloth, but the gag refused to budge.

She changed her strategy, thumping her shoulder against the door, hoping someone would hear the noise and investigate. Unfortunately, the tablecloths covering every patch of the infernal cupboard muffled any sounds she made.

Brianna growled in frustration. She couldn't expect help from outside.

Or could she? Troy had tied her hands behind her back, but she reached around as far as she could. Her fingers brushed her pocket. A little farther, and they grazed her phone.

Painstakingly, bit by bit, she inched the device out of her pocket until she gripped it awkwardly in her bound hands. Now, how could she use it?

Calling was out of the question since her gag prevented her from speaking. By twisting her body to its maximum flex, she could just see the screen in her bound hands. She called up her messaging application and typed a message to Devon Moore.

Troy Winchester is the killer.

She pressed send, then prepared to tell him where she was trapped. But before she could finish the text, the phone slipped out of her sweaty hands. It fell to the floor with a dull thud against carpet. She made an incoherent growl of frustration and squatted to retrieve it.

The space was too tight, and her bonds unbalanced her. She fell against the side and wedged into place, unable to move to right herself. She groaned and wriggled to fetch the phone, but her movements kicked it out of sight under a tablecloth.

She rolled slightly to the side, and for the first time, she felt something that was not soft or made of fabric.

Maybe it was a broken folding chair or some other piece of metal, but the edge was jagged. Brianna wriggled around until her wrists rested against the sharp metal and started to scratch the cord against it.

It was a slow process. She rested occasionally when the effort grew too much. She despaired at ever breaking free—extension cords had metal wires once she'd broken through the plastic outer covering—but she had nothing else to try, and she had no intention of giving up.

Footsteps outside preceded the door flinging open. Brianna blinked with watering eyes at the light streaming in.

"Just checking that you're still tied up," Troy's voice floated down from above. "The judging is almost done. Not long now. We'll figure all this out shortly, I promise."

A wave of rage heated Brianna's chest. Quicker than thought, she lunged out with her bent legs and kicked Troy's right knee.

He cursed and clutched his leg. "Just stay in there," he ground out and pushed her legs painfully when he slammed the door shut.

Brianna squeezed her eyes tight and took deep, wheezing breaths through her nose. Then, she returned to her fruitless task of sawing through the extension cord. Every so often, metal would catch the tender skin of her wrists. Her hands grew slick with blood.

Her phone rang three times in succession. Was Devon trying to call her? Brianna sawed with greater determination.

Voices spoke in muffled tones outside the closet door. Brianna stopped what she was doing, held her breath, and listened.

"Final discussions of the wines," a man spoke loudly. "Can someone get the door, please? We don't want the vintners to hear us deliberate."

"Especially since there might be a few surprises this year." Esme must have been standing in front of the cupboard, because her low voice carried through the wood and fabric easily. "What did you think of exhibit D-4?"

"Easily the best," another man said. "No question."

"I'll be promoting that one to my friend David Blaise," Esme said. "The celebrity chef in Los Angeles. He trusts my taste, and he's always looking for new wines to showcase in his highly successful restaurant."

Brianna rolled her eyes at Esme's typical name-dropping. Then, she raised her feet and kicked the door. The thud was barely loud enough to hear. The main speaker droned on about the competition. Brianna kicked again with more force.

Come on, Esme, she thought. *Listen.*

She kicked again, and the thump was louder this time.

"Did you hear something?" Esme said to her companion.

Brianna kicked again.

"Yes," the man said. "From behind us."

"If you have something to share with everyone," the main speaker said in an aggrieved tone, "please, speak up."

"Sorry," the other man said.

Brianna thumped again. Footsteps walked closer. The door opened, and a blinding light shone down on her. This time, the shocked face of Esme appeared.

"Brianna," she exclaimed. "What on earth are you doing in the closet?"

The older woman swooped down in a jangle of bracelets, her scarves floating after her on a current of perfume. She plucked the napkin out of Brianna's mouth and hauled her upright. Brianna coughed past her tongue's dryness until she could speak.

"Troy Winchester," she gasped. "He killed Sebastian Merle. When I figured it out, he tied me up in here."

"Troy Winchester?" Esme's companion said in a scoffing tone. Gold-rimmed glasses perched on the end of his long nose, and he'd gelled his black hair to one side. "I highly doubt that. He's been in the main room most of the morning."

"And he's a respected member of the vintner community," the main speaker said. His bald head gleamed under the overhead lights, and a salmon-colored polo shirt stretched over his rotund stomach. He gave Brianna a chiding look. "You must have mistaken the culprit for someone else."

"She's dating the man," Esme said in exasperation. "I'm sure she can recognize him." She untied the rest of the extension cords and clucked at the wounds on

Brianna's hands. She pulled a handkerchief out of her pocket and wiped away the worst of the blood. "Wait, you're saying Troy murdered Sebastian Merle?"

"I am." Brianna coughed again. "I kicked Troy before he left me here."

"He limped by a few minutes ago," a man wearing jeans and a fedora said from the far side of the room. "He looked rough."

"Good," Brianna said with feeling. She crawled back into the closet and pushed around tablecloths until she found her phone. "I'm going to call the police. But we need to make sure Troy doesn't run."

Esme's companion laughed. "He's not going anywhere until the results of the competition are announced. I've never seen anyone so avidly interested. He'll stick around."

"No one warn him," Esme said firmly. "We need to keep him here until the police arrive."

"But the schedule," the main speaker warbled. "We must stick to the schedule."

"As long as we guard the exits, we can prevent him from leaving," Brianna said. "You should all be visible during the winner announcements. I can gather reinforcements for guard duty, if I can leave this room without anyone seeing me."

"The window is large," said Esme. "You're young. You can climb out and walk around to the front door from the outside. I'll distract Troy once we leave this room."

"Good." Brianna ignored Devon's missed calls and dialed his phone number. She could have dialed emergency and found the next available officer, but after Troy… She desperately wanted to hear the voice of someone she trusted.

"Brianna," Devon said urgently. "What did you find out?"

"He confessed to me," she said faintly. "Then he tied me up and shoved me in a closet. I only just escaped. He's at the community hall. We'll detain him here as long as we can."

"We're on our way." He paused. "Don't do anything rash."

Brianna hung up and nodded resolutely at Esme, who returned her gaze with a look of steel.

"Point me to the right window," Brianna said.

Chapter 20

Brianna followed Esme to a window at the rear of the back room. The older woman brushed back her flowing sleeves and heaved up the window sash, then waved Brianna to the opening with a grin. Esme's companion peered out the window.

"It's not too far," he said doubtfully. "Make sure you bend your knees."

Brianna swallowed then flung her legs over the sill. It was further down than she'd pictured, and she gulped again.

She couldn't let Troy get away with murder and blame an innocent woman.

"I'll distract him," Esme told her again. "Get the rest of the Gourmand Society to cover the exits. They're all here."

Brianna nodded because she didn't trust that her voice would work. Then she took a deep breath and pushed off.

She landed ungracefully on the grass but miraculously didn't injure herself. She dusted herself off, waved at the judges, and stalked toward the front entrance. All she had to do now was find the Society members without Troy spotting her. Was that even possible?

The festivities were still in full swing. Brianna nervously pulled her sleeves over her wounded wrists to avoid notice. Someone grabbed her hands and swung her around to the beat of the next musical act, a drum circle intently swaying to their own music that pounded as frantically as her own heartbeat.

Brianna extricated herself from the enthusiastic dancer, sidestepped a gaggle of over-sugared children racing around the market, and made her way onto the community hall's front porch. She waved her pamphlet at the volunteers at the door—folded and dog-eared from residing in her pocket for the last hour—and slipped into the coatroom.

She peeked through the open double doors, looking for Troy. Esme had her hand on his shoulder near the judging room. She spoke animatedly to him, but Brianna could only see the back of Troy's head as he nodded.

Esme had taken care of Troy, but where was the rest of the Gourmand Society? Brianna scanned the room.

"Hello, dear." Hilda Button's voice made her jump. Brianna put a hand to her chest and focused on breathing smoothly. Hilda peered at her through her glasses, a large handbag clutched under her arm. "Are you all right?"

"No," Brianna said at once, leaning close to whisper in Hilda's ear. "I need your help. I found out that Troy Winchester is Sebastian Merle's killer, and I need to stop him from leaving this building. Can you and the Gourmand Society help cover the exits?"

Hilda's eyes flashed with determination. "Of course, dear." As if she'd made him materialize out of thin air, Magnus Pickleton appeared from behind Hilda. Hilda then waved down someone across the room.

"What's all this?" Magnus said gruffly.

Quentin joined them, looking back and forth between Brianna and Hilda.

"Brianna solved the murder mystery," Hilda said clearly. Brianna winced at her loud voice—Hilda didn't have the best hearing—but no one was close enough to overhear. "We need to stop Troy Winchester from leaving the competition."

"Young Troy?" Magnus looked affronted. "Surely not."

Hilda whacked him with her handbag. "Just do as you're told, Magnus Pickleton. Stay here with Brianna. Quentin and I will watch the side door."

She chivvied Quentin along in front of her. He looked bewildered but compliant. Magnus huffed but stayed next to Brianna, who tucked herself inside the entry hall out of sight.

"How did you find this out?" Magnus asked her.

"He told me," she said shortly. "Just before he tied me up and shoved me in a closet."

She pulled up her sleeves and showed him her wrists, still oozing blood and ringed with welts where the tight extension cords had dug into her skin. Magnus winced.

"Attention." The head judge spoke into a microphone. "We will now announce the winners of the nineteenth annual British Columbia Wine Awards."

The crowd quieted and gathered in seats around the podium. Troy and Esme sat on the edge, Esme still whispering to Troy to distract him. He held himself rigidly, his eyes fixed on the head judge. He was clearly not taking in a word of whatever Esme was saying.

The head judge continued to speak, but something Esme said must have triggered Troy, for he whipped his head around and looked through the open door of the judging room. Troy must have had a clear view of the closet and its open door, because his face turned as white as Chardonnay.

He leaped up and paused for a moment. The head judge stared at him, and Esme called out. Then Troy darted toward the side door.

Quentin and Hilda stepped in front of the door with their arms crossed, trying to look menacing. Brianna swallowed a hysterical giggle. Hilda was eighty if she were a day, and Quentin was a slight man wearing a red bow tie.

Nevertheless, the sight of an obstacle made Troy turn around. He barreled toward the front door, straight at Brianna.

Magnus stepped in front with his arms crossed, imitating the others, but Troy was too panicked at this point to stop. He ran toward Magnus without halting.

Troy pushed Magnus aside and charged into the entrance hall. Brianna glanced around wildly. She needed to stop him, but how? Surely, something here could act as a weapon.

The only items in the entryway were pumpkins and other autumn decorations. Brianna's eyes scraped over the pile, then she grabbed a pumpkin and lobbed it at Troy.

It smacked into the back of Troy's head with a

satisfying thud. Troy staggered, and the pumpkin split, raining orange goo and seeds over his hair and shoulders.

Brianna turned back to the pile for another weapon, and Magnus followed her example. Brianna grabbed a scarecrow wrapped around a sturdy wooden dowel and brandished the pointed end toward the recovering Troy. Magnus heaved a hefty cornucopia, its plethora of plastic vegetables glued inside, and gripped the curly end. With a yell, he swung it over his shoulder and whacked Troy like he was a baseball and Magnus needed a home run.

The cornucopia exploded, showering the three of them in fake produce. Troy yelled and lunged at them. Brianna fended him off with her scarecrow end, but the look in Troy's eyes made her quail. Anger-tinged desperation filled his expression.

"Take that!" Hilda yelled.

She swung her oversized handbag into Troy's stomach when he wasn't looking. He huffed, all the air leaving his lungs from the blow. With a shout, Quentin grappled him from behind like a dapper monkey. Magnus dusted off what must have been his old rugby moves and checked him, and all three men tumbled to the floor.

A flurry of legs and fists ensued. When the dust settled, Magnus sat on Troy's chest and Quentin on his legs. They'd pinned Troy like a sheep waiting to be shorn, and he looked about as pleased. Distantly, a wail of sirens drifted through the open door.

Brianna knelt next to Troy's face and gazed down at

the man she'd grown to care about. He blinked up at her with wide eyes.

"I didn't mean to kill him," he wheezed. "I told you that. It all happened so fast. One minute Sebastian and I were arguing, the next minute, he was beyond saving."

Brianna's lips thinned. "I believe you," she whispered. "Accidents happen. But it's what you did afterward. You hid your deeds. You tried to frame a man for a crime he didn't commit. You destroyed thousands of dollars of someone else's property. You allowed an innocent woman to be arrested for your crimes." Brianna stared at him, willing him to understand the depths of his betrayal. "And you lied to me."

She stood and looked out the front door, where Devon and Patty raced up the steps, police lights flashing behind them.

"He's here," she said clearly when Devon was within earshot. "I'm happy to give my statement whenever you need me to."

"Troy Winchester," Devon panted as Patty pulled out her handcuffs and grabbed Troy's wrists. Magnus reluctantly heaved himself off Troy's torso. "You are under arrest. Anything you say…"

Brianna tuned him out. Her limbs started shaking with the aftermath of adrenaline. Hilda sidled close and patted her forearm.

"I'm sorry young Troy turned out to be such a bitter disappointment," she said consolingly.

Brianna gave her a half-hearted smile but didn't trust herself to speak. Too many feelings whirled inside her—hurt at Troy's betrayal, fear that she wouldn't recognize a bad apple the next time she met him, satisfaction at a criminal rightfully put behind bars—that she could barely process them all.

Patty marched Troy to the police cruiser once Devon had finished reciting the necessary words. Devon remained behind, and Hilda shuffled away to speak with Magnus, Quentin, and Esme.

"Here you are again," Devon murmured to her. "With another killer."

"This time, I had him in hand." Brianna lifted her chin.

"You did, indeed." Devon looked her over, and his eyes caught on her bloody wrists. His brows contracted. "You're hurt."

"A few scratches. I want to give my statement now, while it's fresh."

"If you're sure." He looked her over again. "Can you get someone to drive you to the station? I don't like the thought of you on a bicycle after your ordeal. I can send another cruiser if you like."

"I can take her." Esme waltzed close to Brianna and wrapped a perfumed arm around her shoulder. "Besides, you'll be wanting to speak to me as well, seeing how I'm the one who rescued Brianna from that terrible closet."

Devon glanced at Brianna, questions in his eyes.

"I'll see you at the station," she said quietly. "I promise."

Once Devon had left in the cruiser with Patty and Troy, Brianna heaved a sigh of relief. They'd caught the killer. Sure, the mystery had upended her entire life and its trajectory had altered considerably. Despite that, justice would be served.

Esme tugged Brianna outside toward her sleek silver sedan. To her surprise, Quentin, Hilda, and Magnus trailed along behind them.

"Are you all coming?" she asked them.

"Of course." Magnus puffed up his chest. His beard waggled at her. "They'll want our statements, too, I have no doubt. Did you see my blow to Troy with the wicker thing?"

"And I took him to the ground," Quentin piped up, his bowtie askew.

"I walloped the lad until he couldn't breathe," Hilda said proudly. Brianna hid her smile as she helped the elderly woman into the front seat with her handbag weapon.

"I saw you all," Brianna said as she settled into the backseat with Magnus and Quentin. "Thank you so much for coming when I called. It's a wonderful thing to have friends I can trust."

"Don't give Troy a second thought," Esme advised. She turned to back out of the parking spot. "And don't swear off men because of one bad apple. He's the minority."

"Esme," Magnus said suddenly. "Who won what in the competition? I wanted to know, then Troy ruined everything for us."

"Oh, yes." Hilda pulled out a sock and darning needle from her handbag and got to work. "Tell us who won."

"There are lots of wine-specific awards, but first place for overall quality went to Grapes of Wrath Winery," said Esme.

"They're not even on the islands," Quentin said indignantly. He pushed his glasses up his nose when his scowl jiggled them out of place.

"It's a blind taste test," Esme reminded him. "Second place overall went to Shelley Bins."

"The apprentice vintner from Orca Vineyards?" Brianna asked.

"The same," Esme confirmed. "Apparently, she's been working on her own project on the side, and Sebastian never knew about it. It's a fine product, and she'll be going places, that's for sure."

"What about Duchess Row?" Brianna asked.

"Surprisingly, Duchess received an honorable mention for interesting flavors. It was difficult to judge them next to the grape varietals, but the wines were very drinkable with a good nose." Esme pulled into the parking lot of the municipal services and turned off the car. She looked at Brianna. "Time to relive that whole mess, Brianna. Are you ready?"

Brianna looked at her Gourmand Society friends, all willing to stand up for justice alongside her.

"Yes," she said simply. Despite the cracks in her heart from Troy's betrayal, it was as full as a cornucopia. "I'm ready."

Chapter 21

Macy wobbled on tiptoe on a wooden chair as she pulled a pin from the corner of the café's golden walls. A yellow streamer spun in a lazy spiral down to the ground. Another extended from the opposite corner to a point near the door, and together they had given the dining room a celebratory air during the evening's festivities.

"It's sad to see it go," Brianna said, her hands filled with dirty dishes on her way to the kitchen. Endless small plates and butter knives waited their turn in the café's industrial dishwasher. Luckily, Brianna had rented the wine glasses, and she viewed with satisfaction the full crate with dirty glasses that the rental company would take away for her in the morning. A pile of fabric napkins sat in a bag next to the crate, and Brianna recalled Oaklyn folding the napkins into interesting shapes earlier that afternoon. She'd shown Brianna instructions she'd found online, and the enthusiasm that had leaked out through her uncaring façade had melted Brianna's heart.

"It was an amazing event, though," Macy called out after her. "Everyone thought so."

Brianna dropped her stack of plates on the counter. Oaklyn gave her a long-suffering look from her post next to the dishwasher, and Brianna laughed.

"It's the last batch," she said. "Then you're off the

hook. Thanks for all your help tonight."

Oaklyn released a massive sigh, but Brianna caught her satisfied smile before she turned back to the dishwasher.

Brianna walked back into the dining room, where Macy had finished pulling down the decorations she'd so carefully placed there earlier in the day. Brianna yawned. It had been a long evening of entertaining—and it was late—but the warm lights of the café held the darkness outside at bay.

"It was so cute," Macy declared, her hands on her hips as she surveyed the now-tidy dining room. "The café always looks great, but the streamers turned it from classy to party."

"This was my café's big event of the season, and I think we nailed it."

"I can't decide if my favorite part was the amazing selection of local cheeses and wines, the general buzz of so many customers, or the Gourmand Society's special feature." Macy laughed. "They were pretty great."

Brianna shook her head at the memory, but the corners of her mouth twitched upward involuntarily. Hilda, Magnus, Quentin, and Esme had ruled supreme over one corner of her café. Quentin and Esme had acted as cheese sommeliers, passing out samples and recommending pairing suggestions. Hilda had passed around chutney from the Bumblebee's kitchens, dropping a spoonful onto whatever plate happened to be passing by. And Magnus had lectured about the superb qualities of the local cheese to anyone who would listen.

Their entertainment value was unparalleled, and despite the Society throwing a small wrench in her vision for the evening, Brianna couldn't help admitting that they had livened up the event in a way that only they could.

Brianna patted a seat at one of her café's round tables and sat at the adjacent one. With a sigh, Macy flopped down and clutched the wine Brianna had poured for her. There were still a few bottles left over from the event. She saw no point in wasting them.

"Thanks for all your help today." After Macy waved the thanks away, Brianna continued. "No, I mean it. You've been great—not just today, but over the past few months—helping me settle in, the investigations, the café, everything."

"It's not too hard being your baking tester." Macy chuckled. "I'm happy to do my part. And I'm grateful to you for giving Oaklyn a chance."

Brianna grinned then sobered. She lowered her voice. "I was thinking about Oaklyn and her boy troubles, how Rob stood her up. There were so many red flags, and she couldn't see any of them. I chalked it up to youth and inexperience, but then look what happened." Brianna waved at herself. "Troy's lies completely took me in. I mean, if I can't see that I'm dating a killer and a liar, how much life experience do I need, exactly? Will I have it all figured out by the time I'm eighty?"

"Probably not." Macy sighed and rubbed Brianna's forearm consolingly. "The fact is, he was a great guy, at least on the surface. You can't be a mind-reader.

Sometimes you just have to take a chance on people. But you can't know everything."

"Seriously, though, looking back, all the red flags were there." Brianna pushed around her wine glass with nervous fingers. "He wouldn't talk about the murder with me, he was anxious beyond reason during the past few weeks…"

"Don't beat yourself up," Macy said gently.

"Honesty is the only thing I want in a man," Brianna declared. "In anyone, really. I can overlook weird laughs, odd looks, snoring, chewing with his mouth open, as long as he's honest."

"Chewing?" Macy squinted at Brianna. "Really?"

"It's correctible. Dishonesty is hard to cure."

Brianna sliced off a piece of Camembert that she'd set out for the two of them.

"Oh, is it time to dig in?" Macy said, sitting upright. "I was waiting until we were completely done tidying."

"Close enough. Don't wait on ceremony on my account." Brianna brought the cheese-covered cracker to her mouth and chewed slowly. "Mmm. I picked the best occupation, didn't I?"

"I love my little ragamuffins, but endless cheese is hard to beat." Macy picked up her wine and sipped it. "Whimsical Wines is okay, but the wines from Orca Vineyards are definitely better."

"It must be the burned sage flavor coming out," Brianna teased.

Macy held up her glass. "To Sebastian Merle, may the ornery old codger rest in whatever peace he deserves. And to truthful boyfriends, wherever they might be."

Brianna clinked her glass with Macy's, wondering if the last reference in her friend's toast even existed.

"I'm glad you can put all this behind you now." Macy put her glass down on the table. "It's time to focus on new things. Rumor has it that a big magazine from the mainland wants to do an in-depth article about Driftwood Island—its history, its culture, its secrets—and they're going to send a journalist over to plumb the depths. I don't know when, maybe in a week or a month, it all depends on when they have room in their magazine. Exciting, though. You'll have to make sure the café is shining bright for that."

Someone tapped sharply on the glass of the café's door. Brianna jumped and turned. Devon Moore stood outside in civilian clothes with a soft-sided cooler slung over one shoulder. In his other hand, he held the reins of his glossy black horse Sarge, who nuzzled his side.

"It's late. I should get home," Macy said hurriedly. She gathered her purse and slung it over her shoulder. "Oaklyn, time to go!"

Oaklyn emerged from the kitchen and sauntered toward her mother. Brianna followed Macy and her daughter to the door, a little flummoxed by Macy's hasty departure and Devon outside.

Macy flung open the door with Oaklyn shuffling after her. "Good evening, Corporal Moore," she said brightly. "Lovely weather."

"Ah, yes." He shifted awkwardly. "A nice autumn so far."

"Do you always carry a cooler around with you?"

Oaklyn asked bluntly. "Does it have beer in it? I thought people weren't supposed to drink on the street. A cop should know better."

"Oaklyn," her mother hissed, "don't be rude."

"It's not beer," Devon said quickly. He opened the lid and tilted the cooler their way. A pungent scent greeted their noses. "I promised Brianna I'd bring her some smoked trout."

"Wonderful," Macy said. "Well, we can't stay. Good night, both of you."

She ushered her daughter toward her little red hatchback. Oaklyn turned to look at Brianna. *Kingfisher*, she mouthed with a smirk.

Brianna pursed her lips and ignored the girl's comment. "Come in if you have a minute. Can you tie Sarge to the streetlight? I'm sure I have a carrot somewhere. And thanks for the fish. It looks amazing. I should pop it in the fridge."

"Sorry I couldn't come to your event tonight," he said. "Work, you know."

"I understand." She grinned at him. "Someone has to make sure people park in the correct spots."

Devon's cheeks colored at her reference to their first meeting, when he'd almost given Macy a parking ticket. His mouth twitched. "Someone has to do it. Otherwise, parked cars would take over the town, and then where would I ride Sarge?"

Brianna chuckled, leaving Devon and hurrying to the kitchen. She rummaged in the fridge for a carrot. Then she grabbed a plate, took a fillet out of the bag Devon had handed her, and cut it into cracker-sized pieces.

When she returned to the dining room, Devon was examining a framed photograph of a ripe cheese wheel.

"Camembert," she explained. "I have some in real life, too. Let's see if it goes well with smoked fish. Our own little charcuterie plate."

After she'd delivered the carrot to the appreciative lips of Sarge, they sat across from each other at the cloth-covered table that Macy had recently vacated. Brianna shuddered slightly at the brush of fabric against her legs, then she sternly told herself to get over it. A phobia of tablecloths would be hard to explain, even if she had an excellent reason for it. Besides, she could never hate the café's table coverings, with their cheery yellows and cheese patterning. The trauma would fade… eventually.

As if he could read her thoughts, Devon asked, "Are you doing all right? This morning's capture was a huge ordeal for you."

"I'm good. Thanks for asking." Brianna smiled at him, then her expression turned brittle. "I'm less affected by the events of the fight, and more because the guy I was dating killed someone and then lied to me. That's the hardest part to get over."

"I'm sorry he was unworthy. You deserve so much better than that."

Brianna's cheeks warmed at Devon's sincerity. She placed a piece of fish on a cracker and put it in her mouth to cover her feelings.

"Mmm. This is really good," she said after swallowing. The pungent smokiness beautifully enhanced the delicate flavors of the fish, and the contrast between soft fish and crunchy cracker melded perfectly in her mouth. "Thanks for bringing me some. What a treat."

Devon opened his mouth to reply, then his phone beeped with a text. He pulled it from his pocket and read the message, and his smile faded.

"I almost forgot—I'm meeting up with Cecelia now." He stood and picked up his cooler.

"Of course." Brianna dusted her hands and accompanied him to the door, ignoring the twinge of disappointment in her gut. It had been nice visiting with Devon, however briefly. She enjoyed having friends in this town, relative newcomer though she was.

Devon turned at the door, and his gaze sought hers. "But I'll see you Monday," he said.

Brianna frowned. "What's happening Monday?"

"Scones," he said with a blink of surprise. "The detachment would never forgive me for forgetting their scones."

Brianna laughed and waved as Devon rode Sarge away through the cool night. She shivered and wrapped her knitted sweater closer around her waist. The coolness in the air brought the promise of winter, but Brianna wasn't worried. She had warm friends, a vibrant cheese café, and a town that pulled together to make sure justice was served. Despite her disappointment with Troy, she would embrace the future with open arms.

Acknowledgements

Thanks to my editor Sara Lawson and beta readers Gillian Brownlee and Michaela for their careful eyes on the manuscript. Also, thanks to Costa Gavaris of Rigour and Whimsy for his help. Any wine-related discrepancies are my own.

About the Author

Michelle Ford adores books, cheese, and the West Coast of Canada. Tying these all together in a cozy mystery bundle was a tasty treat she couldn't resist.

Michelle also writes urban fantasy novels under the name Emma Shelford. Visit emmashelford.com to find out more.